Hour of the Black Wolf

Sheriff Gus Dudgeon finally has a witness who can identify the masked outlaw Black Wolf, who has terrorized Autumn Jericho for years. Gus must keep the witness safe until a wanted poster artist arrives and a likeness of the outlaw sketched. It should be simple. But Black Wolf has influence across town and Sheriff Dudgeon finds he can trust no one but his closest men.

While the sheriff is protecting his witness, Black Wolf sends Big Jim Deal to prevent the artist arriving. But it seems Big Jim is also having trouble trusting his men, and there are people lurking in the shadows and willing to help Dudgeon, too.

With tensions rising, time running out, the hour of the Black Wolf is at hand.

Hour of the Black Wolf

Mark P. Lynch

A Black Horse Western

ROBERT HALE · LONDON

© Mark P. Lynch 2012
First published in Great Britain 2012

ISBN 978-0-7090-9636-8

Robert Hale Limited
Clerkenwell House
Clerkenwell Green
London EC1R 0HT

www.halebooks.com

Typeset by
Derek Doyle & Associates, Shaw Heath
Printed and bound in Great Britain by
CPI Antony Rowe, Chippenham and Eastbourne

CHAPTER 1

The powerful locomotive was cutting an iron path around the rim of the flat prairie plain, its early morning shadow racing beneath a snake of twisting smoke, when the sound of excited voices hauled Sam Sloane from the depths of sleep. It had been the monotonous *gu-dum, gu-dum* of the wheels over the rails that had lulled Sam to dreams, but now children – a boy and girl – were talking quickly and loudly. And it sounded like they were right beside Sam's ear.

'Let me see,' the boy was saying.

'No. I saw first. They're mine.'

Eyes adjusting to the dim morning light of the carriage, Sam saw what they were arguing about and placed a hand on the papers spread across the small table. Must've fallen asleep doodling and hadn't cleared them up. That wasn't good. Given the circumstances, it was downright dangerous.

'No,' Sam said firmly. 'They're mine.'

'Did you draw them?' the little girl asked from

across the table. She was perched wide-eyed on the edge of the seat, impressed at Sam's drawings.

'I did. And I'll kindly ask you to hand that back.'

The girl passed the sheet she held over, but not before studying the image on the paper – a sketch of the interior of the carriage, economic strokes depicting seats and overhead racks stacked with luggage. 'Gee. You're really good.'

'That's kind of you to say,' Sam said, taking the drawing and putting it with others showing life during the journey so far, back when there were more carriages, more people aboard. Lighter now, the train was down to a couple of passenger carriages and a goods van. Sam sighed. The drawings were doodles really, hard to get out of the habit of producing.

'Will you show me?' the girl asked as Sam was about to clear them away.

'I beg your pardon. Show you what?'

'More pictures, how you draw like that.'

'Well, I think that maybe you ought to show some manners first, little lady, and allow me time to wake up. I don't believe handling other people's property without their permission is a good way to make an impression.'

'Sorry,' the girl said, chastened. She stepped into the aisle, stood awkwardly with her brother. Sam figured them for siblings, they were so alike; button noses, blue eyes, lightly curling dark hair. The brother tried to shield himself from Sam by edging behind his sister.

'Come out from there,' Sam told him. 'Anything you'd care to add?'

'I'm sorry too, I guess,' his voice barely audible above the clatter of the train wheels.

'Apologies accepted,' Sam said, wondering how hard on kids you could be out here.

The carriage was half full, many of those occupying the booths lay dozing, hats on the tables separating the facing seats. Men and women of varying ages. There were no obvious clues about which might be the children's kin and Sam didn't care to find out. Poking around in others' affairs wasn't on the itinerary. Sam had been warned to keep a low profile.

'Don't you think you should run and find your parents?' Sam said, stifling a yawn.

'But we want to draw. Faces and things, like you've done. Will you show us?'

Sam softened. After all, the kids must be bored by now. It had been a long trip, riding all of yesterday and then overnight too without much of a break. This was big country they were steaming through the heart of, and while the train had eaten up mile after mile of it and their journey should end today, it still felt like there was more than enough terrain left to cross. Any distraction would be welcome. 'Show you what, sweetie?'

'How to draw like that. I want to be as good as you.'

7

'. . . Well, all right. I'll show you a few simple things. Hop back up on that seat opposite me, the pair of you. We've some paper here, and a pencil.' Sam had been about to stow the sketches away, but instead selected a sheet containing an illustration of one of the conductors – a thin-faced man with long moustaches – and turned to the blank side and began curling strokes on to the clean paper. 'And we start out by. . . .'

Sam drew. One line aided another, criss-crossing strokes brought depth and shadow to the drawing. The children watched as form and familiarity took shape. 'That's us!' the boy gasped after a while.

'It is. Yes. Glad you can see that.'

'Golly,' the boy said. 'Hetty, look.'

But the girl's attention was fixed out the window. When Sam asked what was wrong, and didn't she want to see the drawing now she'd asked for one, the girl turned palely from the view beyond the glass. Her voice trembled. 'Men on horses, and they've got guns.'

Shooting a look outside and then eyeing the incriminating illustrations on the table, Sam's immediate thought was, *Oh God, Jackson Ellroy was right. This is too dangerous. They've found me. And now they're going to kill me.*

Will Tayling woke just before sunup with a crick in his neck and a bad sense of things unravelling.

It had been his intention to wake earlier than he

had, but he'd slept over and there was movement around the camp by the time he kicked off his blanket. Beyond the top of the spruce trees to the east, the sky was pinking with dawn, while to the west the last of the night's stars were fading to invisibility. There wasn't a cloud to be seen.

Will sat up and tugged on his footwear, mindful of the throwing knife sheathed in the back of the left boot. He was thinking about the man who'd ridden in to join the gang last night. There was potential danger there. He couldn't afford to let it go and hope for the best.

'Hey, the Quiet One's awake,' a voice said from over by the fire and cracked out a laugh. 'You fancy some bacon, Quiet?'

That's what they called him. Since Deal had taken him on a couple of days ago – 'Strictly on a trial basis, you understand. You don't follow my orders, do as I tell you, we cut you loose' – Will had kept his head down and engaged in little conversation. Keeping it light and friendly, but not speaking unless he had to, he'd watched the play of the gang, listened for titbits of information he might find useful. Calmly getting on with whatever task he was put to, it suited him to play the role they'd fashioned for him as the Quiet One.

'You sure you're able to keep up with us?' Deal asked Will now, as Will passed up the offer of bacon. Big Jim Deal looked him over like he was a sickening hog that might need putting to slaughter early.

'Because if you're not, you'd better leave now. Ain't room for a freeloader. There's plenty of hard riding ahead. Tough work that could turn a man's stomach if he's not of a mind for it. Told you when I let you in, I run to a tight schedule. It's the way I do it, the way my employer does it. The way we both like it.'

Will's ears perked at this. It was the first time Deal had openly referred to his employer. But now wasn't the time to press him on it. Brushing out the creases in his pants, Will stood up, the only man among the group tall enough to look levelly into Jim Deal's eyes.

'I hear what you're saying.'

'And?'

Will brushed a finger along his chin. It wasn't that Jim Deal drove his men hard; Will was used to hard riding and rough conditions. No, Will had woken late this morning because he'd had to travel a long way in a short time to be sure of getting hired. Because the gang was moving as soon as he'd been taken on, he was still feeling the aches from his travels; the tiredness had caught up with him last night. Clear-eyed, he met Jim Dale's gaze now.

'There won't be a problem,' Will said, voice little more than a whisper but carrying just fine.

Deal's eyes were like shale. 'Make sure to mind you do what you gotta do, then get ready to saddle up. Time's not on our side and we gotta make where we're headed to fast.'

Will nodded, and reached for his hat, angling it the way he liked, so that when it finally rose, the sun only caught the bristles of his jaw, keeping his eyes in shadow. He hitched up his pants, turned to go make his morning water, following the diminishing figure of French Henry along the animal path to the beck, there to do what he had to do.

'Shoot, but if that ain't more bad luck we don't need,' Jim Deal said, looking down at French Henry. 'You just come on him like this?'

'Way I found him,' Will said, standing back to let him see his colleague's body.

Deal sank to his haunches, not touching Henry, who lay sprawled half in and half out of the beck, a host of dangerous rocks around him. Deal was getting his boots wet, and the legs of his pants, as he recreated the scene, figuring how French Henry got to be like he was.

'I reckon the way he's laid here, he'd have come on down the same trail we just used. Half asleep, the sun not fully up, he lost his footing. Bashed his head as he went down. Probably never even knew what hit him. Either died straight out, or drowned unconscious.'

'He was riding hard yesterday to meet up with us,' slim Carter Hicks said. He was one of the men who'd come down when Will raised the news about Henry. 'Must've been more tired than he realized, stumbling about getting ready to ride quickly.'

'You saying that like an accusation, Cart? Think I'm pushing you all too hard?'

11

'No sir, Jim. Ain't my thinking at all. Just saying, maybe Henry here pushed himself too far, wasn't over all the riding it took to meet up with us yesterday. Wasn't watching what he was doing like maybe he ordinarily would.'

'And now he's dead.'

Will didn't have to join in here, so he played it as he'd done since he'd joined up with the gang. The Quiet One, being this guy they were all calling him, just watching.

Anders Finn, a square-set former logging man with narrow eyes and a heavy jaw, shook his head. 'I don't see it, Jim. Not Henry.'

'You want to tell me how else it happened?' Deal turned on him as he left the beck.

Finn raised his hat, scratched the top of his head, where the hair was thin and you could see his scalp beneath. 'All I know, Henry seemed pretty awake when I spoke to him earlier. And we all know Henry, how careful he was. Something's not right here.'

'Sure something's not right. A man's dead. A good man too. Rode with him often enough and he never let us down.'

'Well, that may be, but Henry lying there like that, it throws up another question.'

'Don't I know it,' Jim Deal said.

'With Henry out, who's gonna set the charges, bring down the rocks? He's the best dynamite guy I ever knew. Who we gonna get to do it now?'

The men stood around thinking. Just when it

12

looked like there might not be a solution and everything had gone belly-up, Finn cried, 'Hey! Look at
him. He's moving.'

Sure enough, French Henry spluttered as he came
partway around, coughing water as he tried to escape
the beck. 'Quick, get in there,' Deal directed Hicks.
'Help him out. But careful. There's a gash along his
head. He's lost a lot of blood.'

Carter Hicks clomped into the beck, Finn moving
to help along with other members of the gang.
French Henry was groaning as the boys got to him,
but the words he was trying to get out didn't convey
any meaning. He was in a bad way; there was no guar-
antee he'd survive whatever had befallen him. His
eyes were wild and rangy, weren't focusing as he was
laid, soaked and dripping, on the grass.

'He don't look good,' Joss Kline said after examining him. Joss had apprenticed as a dentist when he
was young, before he'd developed a liking for inflict-
ing pain in other ways. He'd done some doctoring in
his time too, it was rumoured. 'Gonna have to stitch
that wound in his skull. It'll take a while.'

'How soon till he's all right?'

'I doubt it'll be soon enough for what we need him
for, boss.'

Jim Deal shook his head. He sought out Will
Tayling, waved a fist at him. 'You didn't check to see
if he was alive?'

'No, I didn't,' Will told him. 'Guess I shoulda
done.' Bad mistake, he thought.

'Look, there's three of them,' the boy said.

He still hadn't said his name, and as events turned out, no one ever did speak it within Sam's hearing, not that Sam could recollect anyway. But the kid was right. Looking out the window, three riders were galloping along at a speed that matched the train. Two were darkly dressed, while the third was decked out in faded greys, less stark and threatening than the others. Until you saw the guns. All of them carried guns, long-barrelled Winchester rifles, or else Enfields, as well as pistols on their belts. And that was just this side of the train. There could be more the other side of the tracks.

The girl said, 'Why are they waving their guns?'

'They're not gonna shoot, are they?' the boy asked fearful and excited.

'I don't know,' Sam said. The riders had bandannas or neckerchiefs covering the lower half of their faces. Not a good sign. Sam slid across the aisle, leaned to peer out the window on that side. Before, the view had been of long prairie grasslands, an almost mesmeric, indifferent landscape changing only in the colour of the wild flowers speckled like yellow and purple stars; this side there was more to be made out – a thickly wooded rise of land the railroad was curving around. But that wasn't what caused Sam's heart to lurch.

Three more riders on swift mounts galloping

14

closer to the carriages, all armed, hats pulled down, lower faces covered to the bridge of their noses. One of them swung his rifle toward the locomotive. Sam saw the puff of smoke before hearing the report wing into the air. The bullet flew high – a warning shot. All the same, people aboard the carriage ducked.

'What in hail's goin on?' one man with a dry somewhat strangled voice asked.

'Bandits,' another said. 'Looks like someone's trying to hold up the train.'

'God's teeth, don't they know there ain't a rich person with any sense bound for the rat's end we're headed?'

The connecting door to the carriages burst open and a new voice shouted out shrilly. 'Listen up! Anyone got a weapon, help defend the train?'

The thin-faced conductor with the long moustaches, his cheeks red as embers, stared around wildly, pleading in his eyes as he scanned the length of the aisle. He carried an up and over shotgun as if it were a stranger to him.

'Against how many gunmen?' the man with the strangled voice said. 'Five, six, mebbe more? There's not enough of us can deal with that. Ain't a one of them guys don't look mean as a cougar.'

'Pa, you've got a gun, ain'tcha?' the kid Sam had been sketching said to a homely-looking young man rising out of his seat. He had the same dark curly hair as his children.

'I've an old army Colt of my father's in my

15

luggage,' he told the conductor. 'I ain't never fired it at a man before. Can't say I'm eager to start now. I'm a schoolteacher. But I guess if it came to it—'

'No, Thomas.' A round-faced woman Sam hadn't noticed before put a hand on his arm and tried to tug him back into his seat. 'You're not a fighting man.' She turned to the conductor. 'He can't. He doesn't know how to fight. You can't make him.'

'Ma'am, we need all the help we can get. Those men out there ain't playin'. At best they might just steal from us. But if they get aboard and have the worst of their way, none of our lives will be good for what little living's left in them. Some of the bandits, they're like animals. And they'll take their pleasure where they want it, damn any of your protestations.'

'Oh my word.' The woman put a hand to her chest. 'Thomas.'

'I gotta help,' Thomas said and pushed into the aisle, reaching for a brown parcel suitcase. As he fumbled with the lid, another shot rang out from the side of the train.

Sam peered over the lip of the window. The riders would soon be ready to board. Sam hoped the conductor was right and they *were* simply a bunch of bandits looking to lift any item of value from the passengers. The reality was those men could be far worse than that.

The head of the agency, Jackson Ellroy, back in the big city, had warned Sam about the dangers involved in accepting this commission. And 'commission' had been the way he'd framed it, as if it was something Sam might be familiar with, painting flattering watercolours of women and children against the backdrop of a calm river-bank.

'But it's a real dangerous one, and there'll be folk looking to stop you getting to Autumn Jericho any which way they can,' Jackson had explained. 'The witness is only young, but there's a full description. Got a good look at the man that's wanted, known as the Black Wolf. It could be the breakthrough needed to capture him. But he runs a string of gangs responsible for an awful lot of crimes. He wouldn't think twice about killing anyone who threatened his liberty. So you think twice before saying yes to this.'

Sam had said yes there and then, not giving the dangers a moment's thought.

The conductor and Thomas the schoolteacher, his old army issue pistol raised in his hand, passed by, the other passengers solemnly moving out of their way. Sam saw the colour drain from the young man's cheeks in the few moments it took to get out the door. The carriage fell silent but for the terrible sobs of his wife.

Seconds later, gunfire sounded, and the train rocked to the roar of weapons unloading.

CHAPTER 2

Bucky's a ghost now, Tara-May Leigh thought and tried her best not to start crying again. There'd been enough crying. Ma said she had to stop or shrivel up out of dehydration.

Tara-May clutched her dolly. She'd saved her just as Ma had saved Tara-May, by clinging on and pulling her with her. Tara-May wasn't going to let go of her now. Oh, that terrible night she'd just endured. She could still smell the smoke, feel the burning heat and hear her and Ma's screams as bullets spat into the house, splintering wood and breaking up Ma's prize ornaments. Plates burst in a shower of crockery. Pictures fell from the wall and broke. Then the flames had come, spilling in liquid fire from hurled beer bottles. Ma had saved Tara-May, hauling her into the prickly shadows of the gorse bushes out back, ducking low as they ran across the yard, glad of the smoke hiding them from the bad men.

Mother and daughter had stayed in their uncomfortable hiding place, even though their faces were hot to the touch from the blaze engulfing the house. They stayed there, too afraid to tremble or cough, fearing they'd reveal themselves, until eventually, thinking no one could survive such a conflagration, the bad men had mounted up and ridden away.

It had been a horrible night, in some ways worse even than the night Tara-May's best friend Bucky Wright had been turned into a ghost. But then everything had been bad since she and Bucky had sneaked out to Apple-tree Road.

She didn't want to think on that now. Reliving that night time after time to make sure her story was straight hadn't helped her nerves any. All week she'd been restless, waking screaming, and she'd been promised someone nice would talk to her about her dreams, settle her fears about Bucky's ghost coming after her.

But there hadn't been time for that. The bad men had burned their house down, trying to kill Tara-May because of what she'd seen, what she'd told, and what she could still tell. . . .

She was safe for now, though. Sheriff Dudgeon had promised. And it was true she felt better being in the sheriff's own house and being given a bath to clean up in – right in front of the fire, too, with water specially heated for her. It was a rare treat to have a bath in the day, even if the crackle of the burning logs reminded her of the horrors of last night.

The bad men wouldn't come in daylight, she'd

been told. Maybe they were like ghosts that way. Tara-May snuggled further under the covers of the bed Mrs Dudgeon had made up for her. She didn't believe she smelled of smoke any more, but sometimes odd snatches seemed to curl up and twist into her nose, so that when she tried to catch up on her missed sleep, she'd remember the horror of the fire and jerk awake.

But when she saw the light slicing through the shutters, she knew she was all right. And so was Patsy-Ann, her dolly. Deciding against chasing sleep and being at the ill-whim of the scary dreams, Tara-May listened to the rumble of voices in the adjacent room.

'They found out,' Sheriff Gus Dudgeon said. 'I don't know how. But somehow word got around. They know Tara-May's the witness.'

From eyes rimmed with tears, Karen Leigh, a shapely redhead, looked at the big figure standing by the fireplace. Not half an hour ago, she'd scrubbed and cleaned her daughter in a tin bath right in front of the crackling logs and done her best not to associate the warmth heating up the water in the tin pails with the flames that had razed her house to the ground. Now she was hearing the worst of what she'd feared.

'But what's this mean now that they know?' Mainey Dudgeon asked her husband.

Gus Dudgeon pulled on the stubble speckling his

jaw and said, 'I'm sorry, Missus Leigh, but it means we're going to have to keep you and your daughter in hiding from here on in. I got it wrong saying it'd be best if we just pretended on how there was nothing special about you and Tara-May, that it'd be OK for you to go on living your lives like normal. Stay home, go to school, and all of that. I got it wrong.'

'Hiding in plain sight, you said,' Karen Leigh remembered.

Gus nodded. 'And I'll admit it – thought it'd work, too.'

'It did – for ten days,' Karen Leigh said.

She was a good-looking lady. A real shame for her to be widowed so young, Gus thought. Lately, however, the worry and hardship was slowly being etched into her features.

'Word must have leaked out. Once people figured there was a witness. Well, there was all that activity at the jailhouse, letting the aldermen know, even if it was the bare minimum, so that they could alert the travelling judge to the fact we might have the Black Wolf soon.' He shook his head. 'I shoulda known you can't keep a secret like this. But the new portrait artist's on his way. Another day and we wouldn't have had a problem; we'd have everything set to go. Print the posters up and flush out our mystery gang leader.'

'And now?'

When Gus didn't reply, Mainey said, 'They'll be safe here, won't they, Gus?'

21

'I don't know,' he told his wife. He turned to Tara-May's ma. 'We're isolated out here. Too easily open to the same kind of attack that brought the men around your home.'

'I really couldn't believe they'd hurt a child,' Karen Leigh said. 'Even with Tara-May's friend missing. . . . But now I'm not so sure.'

They considered the kind of men they were dealing with, and then Mainey Dudgeon held up a hand. 'Listen, do you hear that? A rider.'

'Wait here, don't go near the windows.'

The women watched Gus go to the door, his Colt Peacemaker drawn and the hammer back ready to drop. With nimble grace for a big man, he slipped out, pulled the door shut behind him. After he'd gone, Mainey Dudgeon advised Karen Leigh, 'It'll be all right.'

Even though they shared a smile, neither of them believed that statement.

Gus took the steps off the porch, holstering his weapon as he recognized the figure nearing at some speed on the back of a light brown gelding. It was one of his deputies. Taylor Quinn, still green behind the ears, but quick to learn.

'Taylor, what's the rush?'

'Ethan Hague's out by the Leigh place, looking around like you said for us to do, Sheriff.' Taylor reined his horse in and jumped down from his stirrups. 'He was using his initiative, like you're always telling us. So we took Trapper Joe Conner over, see if he could help any. You know how good Joe is at reading sign and following trail. He's like a redskin.'

'Yeah, I know Joe.' Gus nodded. 'What's he have to say?'

'Well, it wasn't the horses he picked up on.'

'What then?'

'Before that. Out in the woods, on the way over to the Leigh house.' The deputy took off his hat, as if it was bad manners to wear it as he passed over this news. 'His dogs got a scent on something and, old Joe, to be fair, he tried not to let them have their head, but they got away from him all the same. Really hauling on the leash. Darn near pulled him over.'

'Where'd they go?'

'Straight into the trees. Me and Ethan went in after them, knowing there wasn't a chance of Joe going to the house to check on any trails if he hadn't his dogs with him. You know how he loves them dogs.'

Gus flapped a meaty hand at his deputy. 'Get to the point. There's a reason you've come galloping over here, and it ain't that you got the dogs back.'

'No sir, it ain't. The dogs, when we caught up on them, they'd found something.'

Gus knew before the young man told him, but he had to hear the words anyway. 'They found a body, Sheriff. A young boy, about ten days dead, we reckon. Some critters had got to him, worried him to the bone in places. But we're sure about it being a boy.

23

And we know how many of them have gone missing this last few weeks.'

Yes they did. They knew exactly how many had gone missing.

Bucky, Tara-May thought, hearing the conversation from her window. For the past minute she'd been listening in on what Sheriff Dudgeon and his deputy – the nice one with the warm smile and the friendly eyes – had to say. It wasn't a good conversation, and the news she heard from it sent chill fingers down the bumps of her spine.

They've found Bucky, she thought. *And he's surely a ghost now, if he ain't already been one since I last saw him. I don't wanna be a ghost like him. Not ever. Not even when I'm old and cain't walk straight. I ain't never want to be a ghost.*

CHAPTER 3

Big Jim Deal's men left their boss brooding and cursing, thankful he hadn't set his eyes on one of them and decided to make something out of a stray glance or misinterpreted smile. It had happened before. Jim Deal had vented his anger by bringing out his fists. And there wasn't nobody in camp as big as Big Jim Deal, excepting the new guy. He was as tall as Big Jim, but not as heavy. A slim, rangy kind of guy, almost invisible dressed in grey; you could forget he was there. And then you remembered he wore his gun-belt on his left leg, led with his left hand, something to mark him out as different from everybody else in the gang.

No, he was tall, the Quiet One, but if you were putting money down on who'd come out of a fistfight the better, you'd bet your horse and saddle and any split from the next job's spoils on Big Jim being the one left standing at the end of it all.

Right now, though, the Quiet One was staying out

of Big Jim's way. He was over by French Henry's horse, checking up on the explosives situation by the look of it, counting out the sticks of dynamite, and wasn't looking to be picked on for a fight. It was just as well. There wasn't time for fisticuffs, and if the gang knew it, so did Big Jim Deal. They'd an urgent mission to accomplish. And they'd just suffered a major setback.

Jim Deal stalked over to where they'd carried French Henry. 'How is he?'

Kline looked up from where he was squatting beside the injured man. 'I ain't no proper doctor, but I think he'll pull through. Keeps coming to, sort of recognizes where he is, then drifts back to sleep. I've stitched and bandaged up his head, thrown some good liquor on the wound to clear it out. That sure woke him up plenty enough when I did that.'

Deal nodded. He'd heard Henry's agonized cry. 'He fit enough to lay the charges?'

'Physically, I'd say no. Not in the time we're looking at, if you want to keep to that.'

'We don't have any choice. We leave it any later and it'll be too late.'

'That's what I figured. So I reckon the best we got is to take all the equipment we need, someone ride with Henry tied to his saddle. He's alive at the end of it, we slap him awake, get him to talk us through where we put the charges and all of that, see how it goes.'

'It has to be right. We cain't risk making too big a

26

mess of things. The boss wants it all just right, so it can be cleared up without too much expense. He's still got his business concerns to think about when this is settled. Right now, he needs time to get to this witness the law's got, so we need to stop that train.'

The sun had just touched the treetops. Dawn giving way to early morning.

'We'll do as you say. But we need another plan, something to back us up in case Henry don't make it.' Big Jim looked to the sky for inspiration. 'And we need it quickly.'

The barrage that struck along the train, shook Sam. Thomas's daughter started screaming, and rammed her hands against her ears, while her brother scrambled into the aisle, making to run after his father. Sam caught him before he made it to the door. 'No, it's too dangerous.'

'My daddy's out there. I can help him.'

'Not now. He needs to think about himself. He doesn't want to worry about you.'

'But I can *help* him.'

'No,' Sam said, placing enough emphasis on the word so the kid could see there wasn't room for argument. 'Your daddy would want you taking care of your sister and ma.'

There was anger and defiance in the boy's eyes, but he knew Sam was right. 'What do you know?' he spat, retreating. 'All you can do, you can draw pretty little pictures.'

That certainly felt true to Sam just now. Outside, the situation was getting critical, and there was nothing Sam could do to change the outcome. The riders had drawn closer. After their initial warning shots had gone unheeded, and the train had carried on at full steam, the bullets struck the carriages and now started winging their way towards the engine. Some hit the cabin, raising sparks against the metal, while others ricocheted off welded joints and uprights, pinging around like deadly bees. The ones that missed their target shot by harmlessly or tore into the first wagon after the coal van, a goods carriage empty of passengers. There was no mistaking how serious these guys were about stopping the train.

Out on the plate between the carriages, the schoolteacher Thomas Stretton nervously levelled his handgun and prepared to fire at anyone who came within his sights. The conductor had left him, saying to make the most out of any cover he could find. 'Stay behind the railings if you can. It might make a difference.'

Thomas doubted it. The railings were half an inch thick at best. The chances of them providing cover were slim. All the same, Thomas took what little hope they offered, sinking to his haunches and steadying himself to loose off a shot should he have to.

'Lord, help me,' Thomas muttered and, almost as if to rebuff any notion of divine involvement, a dark figure floated before him on horseback, aiming a Winchester rifle at someone who must be firing to protect the train from up on the roof.

Thomas raised his weapon, shut his eyes, and pulled the trigger. The recoil flung his hand back, but he didn't let go of the gun. His father had carried it with him during his time in the military, and Thomas wasn't going to lose it now. He opened his eyes, saw gunpowder smoke immediately in front of his face, and then beyond it a dark figure running a dark horse alongside the train, looking incredulously at Thomas and completely unharmed.

'Oh-my-goodness,' Thomas said.

The bandit sighted his rifle on Thomas. In the split-second decision processes working in Thomas's mind, diving for cover warred with loosing another bullet at the bandit. He might at least wing the horse and cause it to stumble, flinging its rider off. But discretion, and perhaps a realistic understanding of his shooting ability, won over. As the bandit fired, Thomas flung himself across the plates.

Surprised not to be weeping blood, Thomas looked up. The bandit had passed by, shooting at other, more competent defenders of the train than a nervous schoolteacher.

'Lucky, lucky,' Thomas said, rising shakily.

He should've known better than to tempt fate. Another rider appeared out of nowhere, a grey blur moving so quickly Thomas didn't even have time to send out a prayer for mercy before a rifle levelled at him and a shot spat his way quicker than Thomas could blink.

Sam hit on the notion of hiding the pictures in the art box. It might only slow the men who were attacking the train by a few minutes, but it'd be more time to think in. If they were looking for an artist, at least by then everyone would know about it, and what sort of fate awaited one Sam Sloane.

'Oh my word!' a woman shouted, and Sam saw why. Somebody was clinging to the side of the train, having lost his footing on the rooftop. Sam detected the glint of a rifle tumbling past the figure, and then recognized the dark blue uniform of a train guard.

'Quick, pull a window down, haul him in,' the scrawny-voiced gentleman urged. But no one moved to help, and by the time Sam had thought to do so, another shot rang out and the guard bumped hard against the train, stiffened, and then fell. Where he'd been only a moment before a dark red stain smeared the window.

'They kil't him, they kil't him,' someone cried, and more than at any other moment in the journey, right from the outset when Jackson Ellroy had issued his warnings about the gravity of the situation, Sam understood just how big a mistake accepting this assignment was turning out to be, whether the bandits were seeking an artist or not.

'Daddy! Please, no, don't let them kill my daddy,' the little girl, Hetty, was screaming now. Sam was praying for the same thing and more too.

Thomas the schoolteacher's son ran to one of the windows, beating it to ward off the bandits. His mood changed to hopefulness. 'One of their horses is running free! We must've got one. I bet it was my pa did it. He shot one of them.'

But Sam had made an entirely different interpretation of the events. To suggest just how right it was, a second horse ran into view without a rider. The clatter of gunfire died and the train began to slow down. 'We've been boarded,' the scrawny-voiced man said over the whining protestations of the brakes. 'Lord, help us all.'

All was darkness for an unknowable amount of time to Thomas. Then there was the pain. He gasped, feeling weight on his shoulder. A hoarse voice urged him, 'Put your hand here, keep pressure on the wound. The bullet's lodged fast. It's gonna need removing at some point, but right now you have to stop the blood.'

Thomas sought the eyes of the grey, shadowy form crouching over him. A bandit, he realized in sudden panic. Worse than that, it was the one who'd appeared out of nowhere on that grey mare peppered with white spots and shot him.

'No, get off,' he spat, trying to struggle.

The pain in his shoulder increased as the grey man held firm. 'I won't tell you again. I don't have time for this. It's your choice. I don't want anyone dying who shouldn't die, it's not my way. I'm trying to

31

help you out here.'

Thomas saw that he was sincere. For a moment the men stared at each other, until the sound of the locomotive's engine changed and the hard squeal of the brakes pierced the air.

'Train's stopping,' the bandit said. Very shortly the locomotive and its carriages came to a halt. There were no more gunshots. Thomas and his fellow defenders had failed.

'What will you do? Will you kill us? I've a wife. My children, they're on board too. God, please say they're all right.'

The grey man shook his head. 'I can't make such promises. I saw two guards fall, and some fool conductor with a shotgun. He'd've done better to stay hidden. I understand his courage. He thought he was doing his duty. But it was misplaced.'

Thomas didn't know what to say. The pain was burning him up. When the grey man released his wounded shoulder, more pain wracked Thomas. But he did as instructed, and bravely kept his own hand pressed where the bandit had put it, hard as that simple action was.

With the train at a halt, raised voices sounded from the carriages either side of them. There were a couple of screams in the compartments furthest from the engine, and a voice shouted, 'Silence,' emphasizing the command by firing a shot as punctuation. The grey bandit stood up. 'Come with me,' he said. 'You go first. Call out to make sure everyone knows you're not armed and that I've a gun pointed at your back. Anyone takes a shot at me, you're in their way. They need to know that.'

Sweating profusely, and swaying as he stood up, as if the blood had left the top half of his body and settled in his shoes, Thomas did as ordered. He went through the door the bandit opened, calling out it was him, don't shoot, don't shoot.

The boy and girl ran to their injured father as he'd reappeared. They skidded to a halt when a tall figure followed. One of the bandits, dressed in grey, hat angled so you could glimpse his eyes and nothing more of him between it and the bandanna over the bridge of his nose.

'Thomas,' the man's wife cried, delighted to see her husband, and then fell silent as she saw the wound his hand couldn't quite keep pressed shut.

The bandit indicated the woman could go help Thomas, and with Sam's help and a couple of women Sam hadn't spoken to on the trip, they helped him to his seat. He looked relieved to be releasing his legs of the burden of his weight.

'Don't let him fall asleep,' the bandit said. 'He needs to stay awake, not sink into unconsciousness. Do what you have to do to keep him well,' he told the women. Then he'd made a quick study of the passengers, pacing swiftly up and down the wide aisle, though he didn't seem to find what he was looking for. He came back, passing Sam and the white-haired gent with the scrawny voice. 'I don't like this one bit,' the fella said to Sam in as close to a whisper as he could manage. Sam didn't either.

The bandits went about their business with ruthless efficiency. The male passengers from the other carriage were herded through to stand in a group, though the women had been left behind with a bandit guarding them. Sam figured the women in this carriage would be evacuated, but no, they were allowed to stay, as were the schoolteacher's children. Two other bandits had joined the one dressed in grey. Both wore black and had bandannas covering the lower half of their faces. One carried a rifle, the other a pistol. For some reason Sam feared these two more than the grey one. He was calm; this pair was mean and edgy, like animals. That made them unpredictable. Creatures of the wild could turn and bite at any minute.

'I want you all to line up,' the squatter one called. 'Form a line down the aisle, the women over in a group at the end there.' He waved his gun at Thomas and his family as they prepared to move. 'Not you. You stay right there.'

Mindful of the weapons, people moved to comply. Beside Sam when all the jostling for position was done with, were the last of the men and the rounder of the women.

The black-garbed bandit who'd ordered the lineup said, 'Here's the situation. We don't have call to harm you.' He nodded to the bloodstain the guard had made sliding down the window, and said, 'Though some folks who weren't prepared to do what we wanted didn't fare well because of that. So you be of a mind to do as we tell you. Now, we're here for one reason. We're looking for a man.'

Sam's heart leaped, eyes jumping to the art box stowed overhead, knowing what was coming next. This wasn't some railway robbery. There was a deeper purpose to it.

'That man we're looking for, some of you might know him, some of you might not but could have an inkling of who he is. He's probably going under a disguise, wouldn't want to draw attention to himself. He's due in Autumn Jericho like you folks. But certain parties have an interest in him not getting to town. That's where we come in.'

The bandit studied the folk before him, saying, 'The man we're looking for is an artist, a professional illustrator. Draws wanted posters, some of which you might have seen on your travels. Though I have to tell you,' the bandit laughed cruelly, 'ain't none of them a good likeness to my handsome features. So don't think there's a reward for any heroism on your part, you can take me down and hand me over to a sheriff or marshal somewhere.'

As he was talking he walked the line, peering into the men's faces as he passed, flicking the barrel of his pistol at fingers, lifting hands at gunpoint so he could examine them for signs of ink or pencil marks, maybe even a splash of colour from a paint collection. The other black-garbed bandit leaned against the far doorjamb at one end of the carriage, with his rifle, while the grey one was positioned by the other door.

'Now if that person I'm looking for – and believe me, ain't no question he's on this train – don't come forward now, or you don't offer him up, I'm gonna start shooting. Beginning with that gentleman down there, for no other reason than he's first in line.'

Sam glanced to the opposite end of the line-up. It was the man with the quivery voice who was first. Flustered, his face reddened. The squat bandit sauntered toward him, lifting his pistol up as he theatrically pulled back the hammer, preparing to bring about an execution.

'Hey, it ain't me, Mister, I promise you,' the old guy said. 'Somebody tell him, it ain't me. I ain't no artist type. I'm a bookkeeper. I've worked in a bank all my life.'

'It ain't me either,' another man said as the bandit walked the line.

'Nor me. I ain't the one you're looking for.'

'You got no cause to shoot someone who ain't the man you're after,' a man said.

The bandit paused, turned on his heel, spurs clinking discordantly. He looked into the defiant man's eyes. 'Oh now, you do not tell me what I do or do not have the right to do.'

With terrific speed and venom, the bandit whipped his pistol into his face. The man staggered but didn't fall. Sam feared he'd fight back and the bandit would shoot him, but he fell silent, any defiance he'd mustered gone as he put a hand up to his bloodied face.

'I'm serious,' the bandit said, and each tread of his boots seemed to emphasize the inevitability of what would happen when he got to the end of the line. 'Gonna shoot every man here if the one I'm looking for don't make himself known.'

Sam saw a glowing light of realization glow in Thomas's boy as he watched the drama unfold. His eyes were narrowing on Sam, and Sam could see the twist of a frown in his forehead and knew what he was thinking. The boy was going to give the game away. Not that it mattered; Sam had already reached a conclusion about what had to happen. Before the kid could speak, Sam stepped forward and said, 'Hey, there. Don't shoot him. He's telling you the truth. He's not the one you're looking for.'

CHAPTER 4

'I want you here, Quinn, looking after the witness and her mother. And see to it no harm befalls my wife either, or you're in serious trouble.' Gus nodded at the deputy's gun-belt, the weapon holstered there. 'You've the authority. Uphold the law. Nobody gets twenty feet to the house without you shooting them. Give them a warning if they're alone. If they keep coming, shoot them dead. If it's a bunch of men, fire a warning shot, see what happens before you start at the lot of them. I'll be back when I can, me or Ethan Hague, and we'll get the witness and her mother somewhere safe.'

'Where'll we put them, Sheriff?'

'I haven't decided on that yet.'

'What about you, Sheriff? Where you headed to now if you're not staying here?'

'I'm gonna go along to where Joe's dogs found the body, take a look for myself.'

'Could be the boy got lost, wandered around, died

out in the woods.'

'But you don't believe that, I can hear it in your voice. Here, tie up your horse around back, he'll start if he hears anything. Should warn you if someone comes by and you're not there. Patrol the house front and rear, but not in any regular order. Keep an eye out.'

Gus left him to lead his gelding around back, then went inside. Mainey and Missus Leigh didn't like that he was leaving, but he reassured them he or one of his men would be back as soon as possible. In the meantime there was Deputy Quinn, and they should make him feel welcome. A couple of minutes later, Gus Dudgeon was racing along the Autumn Jericho road, dust rising in his wake as he took the turn that carried him by Apple-tree Road and on up the Clancy Pass toward what was left of the Leigh place.

He found the spot Taylor Quinn told him to look out for and reined his horse to a stop. Ethan Hague's palomino was grazing the tough grass at the base of a maple tree, tied up on a long line. Gus left his own mount alongside it, patting its flanks as he did so. He strode the tree line, but there were no obvious signs of where his deputy might be. Taking his hat off, he scratched his thatch of dirty blond hair. 'Ethan Hague!' he called. 'Hey you, Ethan Hague!'

An answering cry, with its edges hollowed off by the foliage, echoed and bounced through the upright trunks of the trees. 'In here, Sheriff!'

Gus followed the voice, pushing past brushwood.

He picked up a fresh trail. His eyes adjusted to the green light of the trees. A couple of men had come this way, leaving a path some way in from the edge of the road. It didn't take long before Gus arrived at the scene.

'It's not pretty, Sheriff,' Deputy Hague, a plain-looking, dark-haired man who wore a light coloured hat and was into his mid-thirties now, warned Gus.

'So I've been told.'

'Sheriff,' Trapper Joe Connor said, nodding a greeting to Gus. He was chewing on a cheroot, and though he was only ten years older than Gus, his time in the outdoors had weathered him. A couple of lean hunting dogs sniffed around his feet, on a tight leash.

'Your dogs found him,' Gus said.

'Half of me wishes they hadn't, the state of him. But at least it'll settle the boy's family, knowing what's become of him. They can send him off proper, do right by him.'

'I guess they can,' Gus said, and steeled himself to take a closer look at the body.

'Know what it reminds me of?' Ethan Hague said in a low voice, after Gus had studied the human remains. 'If you take away the damage done by the critters, and look at the wound that ended his life?'

Gus nodded, edging back. He saw what Hague was alluding to. Once you'd seen a certain man's work close at hand you weren't likely to interpret it as anything else. 'What happened to Patch Amory,' he said.

They'd found Amory's body four days ago. No one had expected any danger for the wanted poster artist travelling to Autumn Jericho. After all, that they even had a witness wasn't widely known. Yet word must've leaked out somewhere. Because Patch Amory hadn't just been cut and left for dead as if a bandit had held him up. Patch had been nailed to the old oak that stood beside the crossroads leading off the Autumn Jericho road to the small community of cabins over Rusk way. Nailed, mind you, and not tied to the tree, or else left propped up against it. Nailed. Big old iron railroad nails spearing the palm of each hand. Pounded in with a hammer. It wasn't so much a killing as a public execution.

There wasn't any debating about what had brought Patch Amory's life to an end; the wound was deep and cruel and impossible to miss. The only question arising out of his death was whether or not Patch had been alive when he'd been nailed to the tree, or put up after someone had inserted a wickedly sharp knife into his gullet and torn all the way down through his flesh, opening his innards right down to his groin.

'It's the same,' Ethan Hague said. 'Same person killed Patch Amory did this. That little girl saw him, all right, the leader of the Black Wolves. If we'd any doubt she was making it up. . . .' He shook his head. 'This body tells us them two kids saw him.'

'Only one of them hid and got away without him knowing they'd seen him and the other didn't.' Gus looked at how the body had been pushed into the gaps between the roots of the old tree, saw deadwood scattered nearby. 'You touch any of that?'

'The dogs was sniffin' underneath it when I caught up with them,' Trapper Joe said. 'Had to move it to settle them down.'

'The body was hidden,' Ethan Hague said, getting the way Gus was thinking. 'With just enough room for the critters to get at it, eat it away to nothing. It stays out here through the rest of autumn, into winter, and by the time spring comes around there's nothing but bones left, no way for us to tell how the kid died.'

'Whereas with Patch Amory—'

'They were leaving a message, telling us that this is what would happen to any artist came along and tried making a likeness up from our witness's description.'

'As we suspected, they didn't know about Tara-May the night the boy was caught,' Gus said. 'So they killed him – in that distinctive way, with the knife, probably because the Wolf's got a taste for killing that way – and then his men hid the boy's body, leaving it to the animals to destroy, maybe bring the bones out if they've any compassion for the parents to find next year. That was their original plan. But in the time it took for us to organize Patch Amory coming over to Autumn Jericho, they'd learned there was someone else out with the boy, another witness, and we were looking to get a portrait artist to make up a likeness.'

'They only lit the girl's house last night. Must have learned who she was in the past day or so.'

'Wasn't till news got around about the house burning up that folks in town knew who your witness must be,' Joe said. 'I only learned about it this morning, but there was word you'd got yourselves a witness before that.'

'Someone found out who she was,' Gus said. 'But who?'

He despatched Ethan Hague to fetch Ruberry the undertaker. Maybe a good mortician might be able to make something of what was left of Bucky's face before the parents had to look in on it. It was Gus's task to go speak to the boy's mother and father, tell them what had been found. Gus Dudgeon swore that if he had any say in the matter, he'd bring in the man who'd committed this crime and see he paid the full price justice expected of his deeds. The hour of the Black Wolf would come.

Trapper Joe agreed to head over to the Leigh house, look at the tracks, should there be any. See if he could pick up a trail and follow it. 'After all,' he said, 'it's why Deputy Hague brought me out here. Seems a waste to've come this far only to discover this bad news.'

'Just you be careful not to spread around too much of what you've heard here today. And watch how you go, Joe.'

Trapper Joe spat out his cheroot and urged his

dogs forward. As Gus turned his horse for Autumn Jericho and the grim task of informing Bucky's parents what had become of him, Trapper Joe began to walk the dusty road north. He'd picked up a stick and was swiping it alongside him, ticking away with every footstep. Though it wasn't the last time Gus Dudgeon would set eyes on the man, it was the last time he'd see him alive, and this happier image of him was the one that he'd be sure to try to carry in his memory for the rest of his life.

Oh God. What have I done?

It was the question Sam should have asked after agreeing to take Jackson Ellroy's commission. After all, although there were obvious reasons why Sam was hard to pick out as a wanted poster artist, that wasn't going to last much longer. There wasn't any question but the little boy was about to sell up the information he had – and understandably so, for there was a man's life at stake here. Heck, the whole line-up could wind up dead so the bandits were certain they'd got their man. Sam would've had to volunteer the information up freely anyway to save them. Sam said again, 'He's not the one, mister. He's telling the truth.'

With slow, calculating deliberation, the squat bandit turned around. Sam heard every scrape and squeal of his cowboy boots as he did so. 'Says who?'

Sam couldn't think of a reply, couldn't think of what exactly could save this situation from getting critical. It already was. 'I—'

'Spit it out. You know who it is we're looking for, be mighty nice to know about it. I'm sure these fellows here would be obliged too, save them from getting shot.'

Sam's mouth couldn't form words. Any meaning was lost between thought and the spoken word. Only gaping silence fell from between Sam's lips. The bandit strode forward in a sudden burst of speed, pressed the end of his dirty old Colt to Sam's forehead.

'You've got ten seconds. Then I'm gonna take more demanding actions to get my answer.'

There was a lump the size of a boulder in Sam's throat right now. A mass of thoughts swirled, and Sam feared they could be last thoughts. *Jackson Ellroy was right. I should've thought about this more. I shouldn't have taken the commission. Stupid vanity put me out here, thinking I could do the job when no one else could.*

Sam's eyes closed as the bandit counted backward from ten, skin itching crazily beneath the weight of that barrel and what waited at the other end of it, chambered and ready to explode.

'Nine, eight, seven, six. . . .'

The kid shouted up and Sam's heart felt like it would burst with anxiety, unable to take any more of this kind of pressure. 'Mister, mister. I know who the artist is. She is, that one. Her.'

Sam's eyes opened, and part of her at least took some satisfaction from the uncomprehending glaze over the bandit's eyes as he dropped the muzzle from her forehead. He'd never pictured a woman as a wanted poster artist. He stepped back, before regaining his composure, hearing the kid babble even as his parents tried to hush him up, Sam had sketched him and his sister, she had to be the one, simply had to be.

She saw understanding on the bandit's face. 'Darn it, it's true,' he whispered. Just as the whole carriage seemed to be saying the same thing to itself.

He shook his head, even as he looked Sam over, from her skirt to the high-collared blouse she wore beneath her light jacket. 'Sorry, ma'am. But I cain't let something like this make a difference. You must've been told what you faced. I'm sorry to say, there ain't nothing can change the course of events now.'

He raised the gun even as the other passengers in the carriage either cried out or turned around unable to face what was coming. The other black-garbed bandit, the one with the rifle, made sure no one tried to interfere. Sam saw only darkness, an infinity of nothingness down the barrel of a gun.

She closed her eyes. A shot rang out.

The Wanted poster artist's identity was as much a shock for Will Tayling as everybody else. From the moment he'd come aboard, helping the school-teacher into the carriage, he'd been trying to figure which was the artist. But this? No, Will had never expected they'd send a woman to do the job.

It took a moment before he came to his senses and saw what Joss Kline was about to do.

He assessed the consequences of intervening, marking out the chances of an innocent victim getting hurt in the firing line. There were too many variables to be sure of anything. But if he was quick, and one thing Will Tayling had always been when it came to exchanging gunfire was quick, there might be a chance to come through this without hurting the wrong people.

Kline stood back, levelled his pistol at the girl's face and Will put a bullet in the middle of the bandit's forehead, just below the brim of his hat.

Screams erupted, cries of outrage, but they hushed when Kline fell backward, the passengers amazed the victim wasn't the yellow-haired girl in the light jacket.

A slow sort, it took Wilkie Rush time to evaluate the situation and understand that his pardner had been shot and not the artist they'd come to take down. Will used this to his advantage, leaping forward to narrow the distance between himself and the bandit and thus reduce the chances of a passenger taking a stray bullet. He placed two rounds in the man's chest, before finishing with a headshot.

Will pulled down his grey bandanna and then lifted his hat, all with his right hand, pistol still gripped firmly in his favoured left. 'Quiet, everyone. My name's Will Tayling, ex-Texas Ranger, now freelance lawman, and I'm here,' he said, turning to Samantha Sloane, 'to make sure no one stops a certain wanted posters artist from getting to Autumn Jericho.'

While they took in the news, Will said, 'Any moment now, one, maybe two guys are going to come see how things are going in here. They'll have heard the gunshots. They'll want to know if the man – woman,' he corrected, inclining his head at Sam 'they were after's been dealt with.'

'What do you want us to do?' the guy who'd challenged the squat bandit earlier said. He'd rediscovered his courage now there were two corpses in the carriage, and though he hadn't volunteered earlier to defend the train, he seemed up for a fight now he'd a rifle.

Angling his hat like it mattered to him, Sam noticed, her artist's eye capturing the detail, Will said, 'Just hold back as yet. Stay as you are. And hide those guns. They don't know who I am. When they come in, they'll still think I'm one of them, and I'll take them out quickly.'

'You can do that on your own?'

'I managed these two, didn't I?' The way he said it, Will Tayling didn't think it was a question that needed answering. 'Another two shouldn't be a problem.'

Sam didn't know what to think. About Tayling, about the dead bandits, about the boy who'd given her identity away and was now looking sheepishly out at her from behind his older sister. Whenever she looked at him, he shot his glance away. He was just a kid, she reasoned, but he'd shown some vindictiveness in pointing her out to the bandit. As it was, she supposed, in the big scheme of things it didn't matter. Thanks to Will Tayling, she was alive. She shook herself, trying to get accustomed to the idea.

'Do you have to kill the others?' she asked.

Tayling considered it, calculation moving through the narrow slits of his eyes. He'd thin lips but there was no cruelty to them, and they barely moved when he said, 'I think it's probably safer that way. If we try to capture them and fail, then the outcome's not gonna be pleasant for us. Most especially not for you, ma'am.'

'You were expecting a man too, weren't you? Not a woman artist.' She knew she was right as he pushed by her without saying a word.

'Hey,' a woman watching for activity from the other carriage called in a stage whisper. 'Door's opening, someone coming through.'

Tayling positioned himself by the entrance, with his back to it so that he was looking inside, which left him in a vulnerable position. But there was no time to come up with a better plan. Sam moved into position with everyone else. The dead bandits had been lifted on to bench seats, tucked away so they wouldn't be seen the second these others came through the door. Their absence would be noted soon enough, though, and there was no time to mop up the blood on the floor.

But something else bugged Sam. Something about this Will Tayling, ex-Texas Ranger and now freelance lawman, but what was it? She had the sudden notion it was important but couldn't figure it out, even as she stood alongside the last of the men in the line-up and watched the interconnecting door swing open. The barrel of a rifle poked through.

Too late she realized what was eating her. There wasn't time for her to signal up the problem, though, because a bandit entered, eyeing her and the rest of the line-up carefully.

'What's all happening here?' the voice of Anders Finn said close to Will's ear.

Will moved over to one side, allowing the bandit – another one who'd dressed in dark clothes, though it was mostly dark browns that Finn favoured – to pass by him and move further into the carriage.

'Softening up the passengers,' Will said. 'Try getting them to talk.'

'An awful lot of shooting for that.' Finn shook his head, pushing further inside. He was by himself, Will was pleased to see. Hadn't brought anyone else with him. One of them would be on the steam plate by now, Will was sure, holding the driver hostage. The other? It was debatable. The plan – which Will had helped cook up, his theory being, back when he was with the rest of Big Jim Deal's men, that by getting actively involved he might have enough influence to lessen the loss of life – had always been that when the passengers were split up someone had to keep an eye on the carriage containing the women.

Finn flashed Will a look. 'Where's the others?'

Will shrugged. Though he'd his pistol out, the angle was wrong for him to be sure of placing a fatal bullet in the man. As he stood now, if the bullet didn't lodge in Finn, then it'd exit careening into the women, who were grouped where Kline had first directed them to stand.

Finn glanced back up the aisle, and perhaps that was the opportunity Will should have taken. Slug him on the back of the head with the butt of his pistol, then finish the job off with a bullet as he fell to the deck.

By the time Will understood that's what he should have done, Finn had figured things were more off plan than he'd realized. 'Hey, what's with all the blood if the hostages ain't dropped?' There was a thick enough puddle on the floor, dark red stains on the far door, against which Wilkie's body had flown when Will's shots hit him. 'And you – say, why ain't you wearing your mask?'

Dammit, Will realized he'd forgotten to cover his face. There was no longer any choice, Will had to take the bandit out now. He brought his gun up, and despairingly saw that for once in his life he was too slow. Anders Finn knocked the pistol from Will's hand with his rifle. As the bandit stepped back and braced himself to loose a round from his weapon, there was nowhere for Will to go.

51

'I've always had my doubts about you,' Anders spat. '*Quiet One,*' he added mockingly and pulled the trigger.

Will's salvation came from Sam. She flung herself at the bandit, knocking him off balance. The shot winged by Will into the woodwork of the carriage.

Before Finn had chance to shrug her off and straighten himself for another shot, Will launched into him and the pair tumbled to the floor. There was no discussion amongst the rest of the passengers; the able-bodied men piled into the fray too, and it wasn't long before Finn was relieved of his weapons and overpowered.

'Tie him up,' the scrawny-voiced man said, 'and try to keep the noise down – there's another two of these swine at least.'

The bandit's yells were muffled by someone thrusting a forearm between his jaws, but he wasn't quitting up.

'Thought there wouldn't be a problem, you could handle two of them by yourself,' the guy who'd offered his assistance earlier told Will as the lawman pushed himself to his feet.

'Yeah,' Will growled. 'But there was only one of them.'

'You forgot to tug your mask up,' Sam told him. 'I saw but it was too late to tell you.'

'It's OK. You did well all the same, saved me taking a bullet.'

'What do we do with him?' she said. The bandit

52

was trying to get free, call out for help. 'He's going to make a fuss. Shout if he can.'

Will took up the fallen rifle and drove the butt into Finn's face. At once the bandit stopped struggling and slunk like an empty sack in the arms of his jailers. 'One down,' Will said, 'two to go.'

CHAPTER 5

After she learned the nice-looking deputy was keeping guard on the house, Tara-May slept.

The dreams had found her, of course. Since Bucky had disappeared, they were as certain as day followed night and night followed day. But now there was a change to the usual course of events. Before, Bucky had been leading her up Apple-tree Road in the angled light of the canted moon, urging that they keep to the shadows. The way the dream-memory normally played out, they'd have their discussion about ghosts, trying to spook each other.

'Ghosts only haunt old castles.'

'You know that ain't true, Tara-May.'

She did, but wasn't going to let him frighten her. 'Where's this ghostie rider then?'

'I tell you, it's no lie. I seen him come this way. Heard him pass by our cabin so many nights. But when I've gone out to have a look, there ain't never been no one there. It's like all you can hear is the horse, running off into the dark. I didn't think I'd ever see him – or that if I did, well my heart, it would've stopped beating.'

Tara-May poked his arm. 'You ain't dead.'

'Saw him all the same. Tonight. A shadow, flowing cape curling up after him. He rode a pitch-black stallion dark as night.'

And then they were on Apple-tree Road, way beyond any houses, seeking the ghostly rider. Crickets sung in the grass, bugs made the sky buzz with their fluttering wings, and it was so dark. Without the moon they'd have been like blind men. Despite knowing there weren't such things as ghosts – because if there had been ghosts surely her dear departed daddy would've come visiting her and Ma, to let them know he was happy in God's own heaven and that he'd always be keeping an eye out for them – Tara-May had been claimed by a creeping dread that spread across the nape of her neck. Then there were the voices.

In the dream, just as in real life, Tara-May and Bucky crept forward, slinking towards the noise. That's when they saw the wolves. There were fifteen, maybe twenty, Tara-May couldn't be sure. They didn't stay still long enough to count them up exactly. Some were on horseback, around the fringe of the circle they made, while others were on foot, horses tied up out of the way. It was the figure in the middle of the gathering that drew their attention.

'*There's your ghost*!' Tara-May whispered.

55

'Hush now, they'll hear.'

But it was true, and Bucky didn't deny it. A figure wrapped entirely in black, wearing an eerie mask that looked like it'd been fashioned after the face of an angry timber wolf, was holding court. Its voice carried oddly in the night, and most of the words were lost on the observers hidden in the darkness. But crimes were being spoken of: past and future crimes.

'It's the Black Wolves Gang! Stay here and don't move, no matter what happens,' Bucky said. 'I'm gonna inch closer, try hear what they say, then we go tell the sheriff.'

Those were the last words she ever heard him speak. All too soon he'd gotten too close and been discovered. The men weren't playing; they snatched him up and dragged him before their leader in his weird mask. Bucky cried out, and one of the men pulled off his neckerchief, not caring that he was showing his face, and stuffed it in the boy's mouth. Tara-May hadn't wanted to watch what happened next, had wanted to run the heck out of there, but she didn't have the chance. The Black Wolf directed his men to scatter out, make sure that Bucky was alone. She'd be caught if she moved.

She hunkered down low, fearing one of them would hear the thumping of her heart. One of the wolves came so close that if she'd had a mind to, she could've reached out and spun the spikes of his spurs. Another followed, making a strange jangling sound as he passed, but he wasn't wearing boots, just shoes and a pair of black trousers that'd been stitched up at the knee. He almost put his foot on Tara-May's hand. She'd have screamed if he had.

But that wasn't the worst of it.

The worst was what happened to Bucky when the men searching for other intruders came back without a catch. The Black Wolf whispered something to Bucky, before stepping off his horse and enfolding the boy in the wings of his cape and dragging him into the trees.

In the ordinary course of events, that's where Tara-May would wake screaming, with the terrifying prospect of Bucky's ghost chasing her, accusing her of abandoning him, even though he'd commanded her to stay hidden no matter what happened. But now the dream changed, and Tara-May lived the rest of her night with the black wolves.

She'd stayed hidden until the gathering disbanded and the men and their horses disappeared into the night. It was only when they'd all left that she prepared to run for help. Quite what prevented her from revealing herself in the bright of the moon, she'd never know. But something told her, Stay still a while, child, she'd swear it. And though the voice in her head wasn't her own and she didn't really remember enough of his voice to say it was her daddy's, that's the notion she liked to entertain herself with and found comfort from.

Whatever the reason she stayed put, Tara-May's life

was saved by it. From the shadows at the tree line strode the Black Wolf himself, a glinting blade of silver flashing with a wicked curve in the moonlight.

Holding in a gasp of surprise, she realized he'd been waiting, hoping that if others were out in the woods with the boy that they'd have revealed themselves. Tara-May looked on, scared to her marrow. She didn't move an inch, tried not to breathe too loudly. The Black Wolf walked into the middle of the clearing and removed his mask. There in the moonlight, his face openly exposed, Tara-May saw every line and detail of his mad, evil stare (and that, she'd think whenever she was told to summon the image again, was far worse than the mask he wore to cover his face). He stalked the clearing, searching further in the ferns where she'd hidden, and she was sure his gleaming eyes could see in the dark like a wolf's could.

But somehow his gaze didn't land on her, and in time he furled his cloak around his shoulders and brought out his horse from the trees, replaced his mask, and rode away, passing close enough that Tara-May felt the thunder of the hoofs pound by. She saw the wolf mask and its savage grin carry on into the night like a scream. And the night, so very dark where its shadows clawed out of the moonlight, seemed eager to take him.

That was where the dream ended for Tara-May this time. But in the very last moment of the dream she heard silken whispers from the woods. Bucky, calling her name, newly dead feet chasing her as she ran under the fiendish light of the mocking moon.

Tara-May Leigh woke screaming to the sounds of gunfire outside the sheriff's house.

'Keep an eye on the door to the other carriage.' Will Tayling was issuing orders. 'Let's find something to bind this man with,' adding, 'Make sure you put a gag in his mouth, so he can't call out when he comes around.' To the guys hefting guns taken from the dead bandits: 'I want you to shoot any who come through that door when I'm gone.'

People were obeying him, Sam saw. The bandit was turned over and trussed up, gagged with his own bandanna. The men with weapons took position, ready to spray bullets at anyone who came into the carriage wearing dark clothes with his face covered. While the rest of the passengers went about what Will asked of them, Sam went over to him.

'You're hurt.' She lifted a finger to his brow, above which a narrow string of bloody beads showed. 'Must've cut you when you fought.'

'I reckon he might've laid a few on me, but it's nothing serious.'

Sam had recovered his hat. She handed it to him now, watched as he straightened the brim, tried to brush off the boot prints, and then put it on, taking a moment to get the angle right, so all you could see clearly was the blue flush of the whiskers on his chin.

'What?' he said, seeing the way she was watching him.

'You're mighty particular about how you wear your hat.'

He grunted. 'Keeps the sun from my eyes.' He looked around, saw where his pistol had fallen, and retrieved it. He broke open the chamber, fed in fresh bullets from his belt.

'You're going after the others?'

'Don't see no choice but to do that.'

'And then what?'

'If the driver's all right, I'll tell him to reverse the train, aim back the way he came.'

'But I need to get to Autumn Jericho.'

'And I'll do my best to see you do. But we can't go by railroad.'

'Why not – you're dealing with these men. If you stop them, there's nothing to prevent us getting to the town.'

'Think so? There's more men like these running ahead of the train, looking to cause a rock fall and block the line. A man called Jim Deal's leading them. Runs his own gang, but it's only part of the bigger wolves operation. Big Jim, he has an explosives expert with him, name of French Henry, and although I messed up his plan somewhat – which is why I'm here now – there's a chance it can still be pulled off and the line blocked. There's more than seven men in that group. I doubt I could pretend I'm still signed up with them, take them all out by surprise.' He shook his head. 'No, ma'am. We can't go that way.'

The reality of the horror Sam was in wasn't diminishing.

'If you'll excuse me,' Will Tayling said. He made an exaggerated show of pulling up his bandanna, and turned for the door. Sam was hesitant as she did so, but all the same, 'Be careful,' she called after him. Whether or not he heard, she couldn't tell.

Will stepped out on to the plates and took a breath. He opened the door of the adjacent carriage and walked in as if he was still part of the Deal Gang.

The carriage was full of fearful women huddled together. The last bandit, Clay something-or-other, Will had never really been sure about his last name, wasn't there. Checking to ensure he wasn't behind the gaggle of women – he wasn't – Will turned over the options. The most likely scenario was that at some point Clay'd come looking to see what was taking Finn so long, had seen some of what was developing and had run for help.

Will slid a window down and looked along the length of the train. Seeing no sign of the bandit on this side, he strode across the aisle, leaned one knee on a seat, and looked out the other. Curls of steam from the engine still ribboned out of the smokestack of the locomotive, and they dipped in loopy hazes by the goods van and the carriage Will had left Samantha Sloane and the other passengers aboard. But through the smoke, Will caught a figure stumbling by the side of the sleepers, heading toward the engine.

'Darn it,' Will cussed, wishing he'd brought along a rifle. He'd opted for carrying only his pistol after he'd left his horse. All the same, narrowing his eyes, he let a bullet fly.

The crack of the report fell flatly on the wide prairie air. Will's bandit stumbled but Will felt it was more out of surprise than because the bullet had caused him injury. To fire again would be a waste of ammo. Will pulled himself back inside the carriage. He tugged his bandanna down, exposing his face. 'It's all right,' he assured the ladies watching him. 'The next carriage on is safe, if you want to make your way over there. Make sure you're careful to call out who you are before you enter it. Just give me a minute first, then head on over.'

Will didn't wait to take questions. He ducked back out the carriage, considered making his way after the bandit on the ground – wondering which side of the train he'd be better attempting that from – and then landed on another option altogether.

Running along the roof, Will came to the end of the carriage and didn't pause; he took a flying leap, unwilling to lose his momentum. He hung in the air, thought he wasn't going to make it, and then slammed down on top of the goods van. He knew he wouldn't catch the bandit before he got to the loco-motive and warned Carter Hicks what was happening, but he was hoping to take some element of surprise to the fight all the same.

Will had been on the back foot from the moment he made French Henry: an explosives expert he'd put in jail years ago, when he'd been a Ranger in Texas. Henry hadn't recognized Will, saying he looked familiar but from where he couldn't remember. Will had known that he'd figure it out eventually. Through his own tiredness he'd made the mistake of not checking on Henry once he'd cold-cocked him down by the stream-bed, and he'd had to come up with this plan of intercepting the train to try to make up for things. As it was, it'd worked out pretty well so far. He'd split Big Jim's gang in two and taken out all but a pair of the bandits.

Now the smoke from the stack lifted again, and to Will's surprise the van he was on jerked beneath him. He tumbled forward.

'They're starting the train,' he told himself. 'Darn it. Looking to hold me off getting to them while they run us to Big Jim's rockfall.'

Sure enough, the train began to pick up speed. Will shook his hand. When he'd gone over he'd hurt the fingers of his gun hand. It was his own fault. Like a fool he'd splayed his fingers, hoping to soften his fall. Likely he'd've been wiser to just take the impact with a shoulder, worry about the bruise later. He could feel the throb now, as though his fingers had been pulled back beyond the extent the tendons would normally allow them to go.

63

He cussed again, rocked by the motion of the train as it gathered steam. This wasn't how he'd envisioned things, not at all. Back at the camp with Big Jim, he'd suggested a small raiding party, maybe only a couple of riders: intercept the train, board, pretending that they'd been chased by Indians, and beg a safe passage. Will the Quiet One telling it in such a way that Big Jim took it all in, seeing the plan as if he'd come up with it himself. 'And you find the artist, shoot him, and you're out of there,' Big Jim had said, filling in the space Will left for him to fill. But then Kline had put his dime in. 'Why send so few? How about six of us run the train, board it shooting and just take out the guy. If he don't own up to who he is, we shoot all the men on board. Problem solved.' Kline: a man to whom the dropping of corpses meant as much as falling raindrops. And look whose plan Big Jim had run with.

Now, pushing up on to his knees, Will flexed his fingers till he was happy he could pull the trigger of his Colt. He might not be as fast as he was before the fall and he certainly wouldn't be able to manage it free of pain, but it'd have to do.

He stood up, finding it harder to keep his balance now the train was moving. The clatter of the engine was streaming back over the roof towards him, as, likewise, was the puffing smoke. Glancing back, he saw where the horses had been tied together after the train had been stopped, diminishing in the distance. He had to do this quickly.

Will started forward, arms outstretched for balance. The whistle sounded, disorienting him. Heading straight into the line of smoke coming out of the stack, he was grateful for the bandanna covering his face. It made it easier to breathe, though it didn't improve the smell any. He thought he heard a cry from behind him, but it could have been his imagination, as it coincided with the whistle going again. Ignoring the call, if it was a call (after all, he'd already established there was no danger from behind, that the two remaining bandits were on the locomotive), he pressed on, and saw he'd come to the end of the goods van. He'd have to jump all the way into the coal truck, right behind the locomotive.

Will stepped back, pulled on the hammer of his pistol so that it was cocked good and true, then ran forward, leaping into steam-clouded air.

He came from nowhere. Carter Hicks had been leaning out first one side of the engine and then the other, looking back along the train in case the Quiet One was attempting some darn fool stunt like climbing along the side of the carriages. So far there'd been no sign of him, but Carter wouldn't put it past him.

Anders Finn had said from the get-go that there was something not quite right about this new recruit Big Jim had hired up in Roma-Lassie. Finn said he'd surely have liked to know where French Henry remembered the man from. Now it seemed pretty clear that this Will Tayling character was involved with the law in some way. And that was probably how Henry knew him. Well, that counted for nothing in Hicks's eyes. You asked him, one dead lawman was as good as another. He felt no reason not to increase the list of badge-wearers he'd killed out here in the wilds.

As Clay kept a weapon trained on the driver and his mate, instructing them to load the coal faster, Hicks fingered the trigger on his old Enfield rifle, putting the stock up under his arm. He kept checking either side of the carriages. *Just have a go*, he was thinking to the Quiet One, *and I'll put you out of your misery, and mine, too.*

Then rearing up out of the coal pit, there he was, feet going out from under him even as he drew a bead on Carter Hicks and showed the deathly hole of his gun to the bandit, rocketing a bullet straight through the insides of Hicks's head.

As Will fell on his backside, the tricky coal sliding away under his boots, he felt the heat from the furnace driving the locomotive like they were the flames of hell.

Carter Hicks's head imploded and though it stood up all by itself for a couple of seconds – more than Will would've ever credited it could – eventually his body went off the running plate. Not quite walking, Will wouldn't swear to that as he rolled on to his side, but it was a darn near thing, and it went sailing out the train to the trackside.

Well, he might've slipped on to his ass because of the coal, but as least his shot had been true, he'd time to think, before a pistol slammed into his face. Through his pain, Will heard the enraged cry of, 'Die, you crazy—'

Groggily, Will looked up to see a blurred figure leaning over him. But the bandit who'd struck him hadn't time to say anything further as a rifle shot flew into the train, striking brass and ricocheting around the little engine room, before zinging away harmlessly.

Clay spun around, lifting his pistol at the goods van, fixing to take care of the more pressing danger now Will was stricken on the floor. As he recovered his senses, Will saw a man outlined through the smoke streaming from the engine. Someone had come to help him, he realized; he recognized the guy who'd been mouthy to Kline back in the railway carriage.

'Fire again!' Will shouted, but the rifleman's weapon had jammed. Now he was an easy target for the bandit. The two-man engine crew were busy with their shot-up dials and valves, and while out to protect themselves, they weren't entertaining any thoughts of entering the fray. Will had to do it all by himself, prone as he was, pistol lost somewhere in the black stones of coal, head aching from being pistol-whipped.

He swung a boot out, catching Clay in back of his knee. The bandit pitched over. The shot he'd levelled at the rifleman on the goods van hurtled into the air. Will grabbed him as he came down, and bashed his head against the metal steam plate. Did it once, did it twice, did it three times. But the man wasn't calling it quits yet, still had his gun. He was shorter than Will but tough. He hooked a fist into Will's midriff. Will gasped, but didn't let him loose. He grasped a hand to prevent Clay shooting him, grappling with him on the metal floor.

They tussled for what seemed like minutes but could only have been seconds. His boots finding purchase on something at last, Will shunted himself and the bandit towards the wall of dials and the gate to the furnace. No one was feeding it coal any more, but the gate had been left open. It was white hot in there, and Will could feel his eyes drying up just looking at it. How it must be for Clay, he couldn't imagine, for the bandit was even closer to the furnace than Will. Will doubted he could take many more seconds exposed to it himself.

Clay cried out and dropped his gun, tried to prise himself free of Will, no longer worried about shooting him. Will saw why. The bandit's hat had caught fire, and the flames were quickly spreading to cover his back too. One of the engine crew found the courage to interfere, though Will didn't know if it was to help Will or else simply to put out the fire engulfing the bandit. The guy in the boiler suit clanged the coal shovel over the burning man.

Will scrambled away before he too caught fire.

Clay managed to stand. The roar of the flames hardly died as he lifted his hands, as if he were burning on a cross, and waved them wildly. He cried in horror as his skin crinkled with the terrible embrace of the fire. Even then he lashed out, hoping to strike Will.

Will grabbed the shovel from the engineer as Clay spun wildly. 'Put it out,' the engineer shouted. 'Put out the flames.'

Pulling back, Will swung, taking an un-Christian satisfaction as the shovel banged into Clay's thick skull. Trailing fire and smoke, the bandit roared over the side of the running plate, leaving behind the smell of burning cloth and cooking meat.

'He's out now,' Will told the engineer, then she shouted to his mate the driver. 'Stop the train!'

CHAPTER 6

Although he hadn't been the one who'd brought about his death, Gus Dudgeon still felt all kinds of a heel for having to pass on the message of Bucky Wright's demise. He couldn't shake the notion that he himself had been the one who'd truly finished Bucky's life in the eyes of his parents. Heading back home at a light canter, Gus's thoughts turned to Tara-May. So much hope rested with her. That girl had been through a lot. Losing her daddy so young, and then her friend as they'd happened upon the gathering of outlaws, and now her house was shot up and burned down. A lot was riding on her being able to describe the Black Wolf.

Gus's friend Will Tayling had set out to prevent one of the Wolf's gangs getting to the new wanted poster artist. So long as it was only one gang, Gus thought, Will had a chance. But many rogue outfits held allegiance to the Black Wolf, mastermind of countless crimes.

Until the train with the artist arrived, Gus would be nervous, anticipating awful event upon awful event. He'd like to get Tara-May into town by then, ensure she saw the artist as soon as they'd hustled him in from the station. Gus didn't want anything going wrong, like it had with Patch Amory. It was still a mystery as to how the Black Wolf had learned someone had seen his face, but once the Wolf knew that, an unsuspecting Patch Amory wouldn't have known to be on guard riding into Autumn Jericho. Patch was another mark in the account of the Black Wolf that he'd have to pay for when Gus eventually caught up with him.

And maybe that reckoning wasn't as far in the future as Gus had imagined. Because as Gus approached the turn-off to his home, he heard gunfire. Distantly at first, so that he might be mistaken, though he'd heard enough of it in his years to realize that he likely wasn't fooling himself now. He lifted a hand behind an ear and listened intently. There it was again; the distant pop and crack of weapons being discharged. Heeling his horse, he snapped the reins, hoping he wasn't too late to make a difference.

Gus rounded the curve at full speed, his horse never losing its footing on the track, and saw muzzles leaning out of two windows of his house. Bright flashes of light came from them, followed by smoke curling in the air. A moment later, he heard the bark of the rifles.

Two men, both in black, were sprawled on the floor, if not dead then injured to such a degree that they soon would be. As Gus charged toward the house, he saw another man. He was behind a water butt, weapon rested across the top, where open water flashed with the reflection of the blue sky, and was taking careful aim at the house. When he shot, splinters tore up around the woodwork of the window one of the rifles poked out of, and the rifleman inside, one of his deputies Gus was sure, had to withdraw and take cover.

Spurring his horse on, Gus 'Yee-hawed,' and entered the fray, pulling out his rifle from its saddle holster. He ratcheted a bullet into the chamber one-handed, and took as level an aim as he could as he rode in. The shot dug into the earth near the water butt, causing the guy to sprawl over. He quickly scooted around the butt, and Gus realized his own mistake, how much of an exposed target he presented to the figure. With his wife and the little girl's lives at risk, he hadn't thought through what he was doing, had acted on instinct. It looked like he might be killed for that now.

Gus was saved the indignity of a sharp and sudden death by the gunman's own reckless actions. By making sure he'd covered himself from Gus's attack, he'd exposed himself to gunfire from the house. Glass burst out of another window, a muzzle followed, and two quick and accurate rounds struck the figure by the water butt. The intruder went sprawling, twitched, and then didn't move at all.

Other bullets still flew though, and one hit Gus's horse, bringing both Gus and his ride down in the dusty courtyard before the house. Though he'd dropped his rifle, as he scrambled upright Gus was able to draw his pistol and target the raider who'd shot up his horse. He was by an old cart Gus had intended to take apart and use as kindling for fires that coming winter. Hidden in the shadows there, Gus hadn't seen him as he'd ridden in.

Though he wasn't as swift a gunslinger as his friend Will Tayling, Gus was, by anyone else's standards, very fast. His weapon was raised and pointing straight at his assailant within a blink of an eye. He slapped down the hammer three times in succession with his left hand while his right took aim and squeezed the trigger.

The final raider was taken out as he turned to flee, running for the cover of the trees now he saw that the attack on the house was a lost cause.

'We'll gather up a couple of horses from the meadow,' Gus told his wife as she took a damp cloth to his grazed arm, the one that'd been injured when he'd come off his horse. 'Mount a couple of them into the buggy and escort Missus Leigh and Tara-May back into town. Do it quickly, before the Black Wolf realizes his plan hasn't worked and the little girl's still alive.'

'I've no objections,' his wife told him. 'The sooner

I know everyone's inside the jailhouse, the safer I'll feel.'

'You need to come too,' he said. 'You won't be safe out here alone. Other men could come along looking for the girl.'

Ethan Hague, cradling his hand where long slivers of wood had lodged from the splintered window frame, said, 'Reckon herding the horses's gonna fall to Mister Taylor Quinn here. I'm gonna be shooting with my wrong hand for a couple of weeks at least.'

'Long as you can aim and pull the trigger, we'll take that. How long you need before we move you and Missus Leigh and the girl out?' Gus asked his wife.

She surveyed the shot-up interior of her home. 'Maybe we'll just go.'

Quinn whistled from his watch at the front door. 'Someone's here, riding a horse.'

'You see who it is?' Ethan Hague asked, telling Gus, 'The boy's got sharp eyes.'

'He's in shadow right now,' Quinn said, tension in his posture as he lifted the rifle in the man's direction. Then he relaxed. 'It's all right. It's only Landon Coyle, the preacher.'

'Oh, I forgot,' Mrs Leigh said. 'I asked him over to my house yesterday, to see if he could help cure Tara-May of the notion Bucky Wright's ghost is out to get her. He must've learned about the fire and come on over. It seems everyone in town knows where we are.'

'The sooner we're at the jailhouse,' Gus said, 'the

safer we'll finally be.'

'No,' a little voice said from over by the door. The adults in the room turned to the child. She said, 'We won't be safe there. If he can send men for me here, burn our house down, and you still cain't stop him, then there ain't nowhere safe.'

CHAPTER 7

Sam scrunched up her eyes, and when that didn't help keep the sun out of them, she lifted a hand to her forehead. She could use a hat, she decided, same as the one Will Tayling was wearing. How bright the day was. Hard to believe that it was only now approaching midday and yet so much had occurred already. This wasn't the life she'd envisioned for herself when she'd left for the city – or *Run away from home on a fool's quest,* the way her father talked about her desire to draw and paint, be this famous artist.

Well, she had what she'd been given her, which was another thing her father used to say before the family rift and her decision to leave. And what she'd been given today were seven dead men: four of the bandits and two railroad guards, plus the conductor whose likeness she'd sketched. A short while ago she'd been in the city, feeling the drag of the relentless portrait work tell on her, while she dreamed of the untamed country and producing sketches she could work up into great works of art. Taking on the commission to draw the likeness of a criminal for a wanted poster had seemed an ideal way of helping her wish come true. But now she felt flattened. This wasn't the way she'd seen her adventure playing out.

'What do we do now?' she asked Will Tayling, the grey-garbed former Texas Ranger, who was sitting astride his horse, a grey mare dotted white like snow had stuck to it. Her own horse was one of the bandits', and she was still getting used to its moods and ways.

Will had stayed quiet as he led her up the hillside, toward the taller trees. Now, as Sam paused to look back through a cut in the woodland, the train was a child's toy, diminishing in perspective as it reversed back to whatever town it was they'd passed through last night to take on more water.

On board were the men and women who'd survived the morning's attack, along with the bound and gagged Anders Flynn, for whom Will had said there should be a nice reward waiting somewhere. Will had gone through Flynn's pockets and those of his bandit compatriots, emptying their purses of coins and handing them to the wife of the shot schoolteacher. It would pay to remove the bullet lodged in the teacher's shoulder, patch him up all right, Will had told her, explaining he'd shot to graze the man, not to kill him.

Already Sam felt vulnerable and deserted, seeing her final contact with civilization puffing away, its smoke trail the only cloud marking the sky. Even that was fading, a sign of how little a mark Man and all his inventions could leave on this vast country. So what would she and Will do now? She turned to him when he didn't answer her and asked again. 'I said what do we do now?'

'Heard you first time,' this hotshot ex-Ranger – who twice had needed helping out, she decided to remind him when he next got too big for his cowboy boots – told her, his face turned not towards the departing train but in the opposite direction, further west, following the curve of the railroad line as far as it was visible. It vanished into trees after another couple of miles of open prairie, and after that, he'd told her, followed a blasted-out cut in a hillside before skirting the base of some mountain or other. Beyond that was the town she'd been aiming to reach that afternoon: Autumn Jericho. Now she wondered when she'd ever arrive.

'And are you going to tell me?' Sam asked.

'Looking to see if we're being followed yet.'

Sam was going to say something but remained silent. After all, Will Tayling had risked his life for her. If he thought there was a chance of them being followed, she ought to let him try figure out if they were or they weren't.

He murmured to himself, then turned, shrugging.

'It'll take longer, I reckon. But as I figure it, we'll be safer going this route than any other. We don't run into Jim Deal's men, and there's little ways for him to cut us off once he realizes we've come this way. By then, all being well, he should be a long way behind us. Only question is will he drive himself on after us harder than we press ourselves.'

'What do you think?' Sam said.

Will knuckled the whiskers on his chin, the rest of his face, as always, hidden in the shadow of his hat. 'That all depends on how well you can ride, ma'am.'

'I've told you I ride well.'

'Due respect, but I'm guessing this ain't the type of country you're used to.'

'Then I'm sure, Mister Tayling, that you'll ease me through it,' Sam said, and without waiting for him to reply, kicked her horse forward, already regretting not taking up his offer to carry her illustrator's box for her. It was biting into the base of her spine as she rode. She soldiered on all the same, damned if she was going to ask him to take it now.

Big Jim Deal commanded thunder. He made the ground shake and rocks fall. Or at least, that was how it felt to him as his ears whined after the explosives charges detonated and the cliff face splintered and fell. A roaring cacophony of tumbling rocks spread over the railroad lines through the pass they called Stratton's Reach, named after the explosives expert who'd first made this break through the rock face for the trains to go through, ten years ago now. When the silence returned, Jim stood up, uncovering his ears, and looked to see the results. He had to admit, it was mighty pleasing to the eye. 'Yee-haw!' he cried.

The other members of his gang, the ones who'd not hitched up with Kline and Finn to tackle the train, cheered as well. Only one remained silent, studying the man he'd been attending to. French Henry was in a bad way. Although Parkins Whelks didn't think that even Joss Kline, the nearest thing the gang carried to a medical man amongst their midst, could have done anything for him, he still wished the sadist hadn't insisted on his opportunity to spread some blood attacking the train.

Parkins didn't have medical training, but he'd once swept up at a barber's when he was a boy. That made him the automatic choice to tend to Henry once Kline left. To his surprise, French Henry hadn't died on horseback. He'd remained sitting mostly upright, his hands roped around the horn of his saddle as Jack Kilkenny led his horse on after his own. At times he'd even come around, though they were fleeting moments of lucidity. It was pure bad fortune that he'd slipped into a deep sleep just as they approached the cut through the rocks.

'Wake him up,' Big Jim had commanded. 'He has to guide us. We ain't got the dynamite to get it wrong. Put these charges in the wrong place, we might mess it up, and nothing come down. Train'll shoot through like there's nothing but dust stopping it.'

'He's in a bad way,' Parkins had said. 'I ain't sure he's gonna come around.'

'Throw some water in his face.'

Parkins didn't think it'd help, but he did it anyway.

'Try slapping him around some. We ain't got the time to play around. We don't stop that train and find that artist, you know what the Black Wolf will do to us.'

Parkins had never seen Big Jim so openly afraid as he was then. He was trying to hide it, but it was there all the same. The big man was scared of what the Black Wolf might do to him. And if the Black Wolf could scare someone like Big Jim, then Parkins didn't like to think just what kind of man *he* was.

He'd patted French Henry's face, harder and harder. 'Come on, you all, Henry. Darn it now, you wake up. We need you.'

As if the gang had been blessed with a little miracle, French Henry's eyes had opened.

'There now,' Big Jim had said, 'we're ready to go.'

When the dust settled, it was possible to see just how good a job the gang had made of following Henry's instructions. To hear him better, they'd had to put their ears right up beside the man's lips. But strength fading away or not, French Henry had come through.

'Ain't nothing gonna pass through there,' Big Jim declared once the cheers and yee-hawwing were done with. 'Now hurry on up, get into position. I want to be ready to board when it arrives. If Kline didn't manage the job, then we jump aboard fast. They won't know what's hit 'em. We shoot all the men if we have to, just so's we can take out the artist fella.'

Big Jim moved swiftly, pointing out places for his men to position themselves in, readying themselves for the arrival of the train. It'd be here soon if it had passed the earlier ambush. Jim was delighted. He was going to do this, after all, fulfil the command the Black Wolf had given him. And while there were no rewards for failure from the Black Wolf – quite the opposite in fact – he was generous when you did something for him that met with success. No mistake, Jim and his men were going to be a lot richer for pulling this one off.

And then Big Jim saw the look on Parkins's face. Discomfort turned his guts.

'He wants to tell you something,' Parkins said. 'I think it's important.'

Big Jim nodded. 'How long's he gonna last?' Parkins shook his head, his features grim. 'You done your best,' Big Jim said. 'Ain't nothing more he could've asked of you.'

'Kline should've been here,' Parkins said, the nearest he'd ever come to challenging Big Jim. The big man let it go. He said, 'Wouldn't have made a difference ultimately.'

'All the same—'

'Kline's the one I trust if there's blood to be spilled. That's why he went to the train. He ain't a man to baulk at the task. Kinda the opposite, don't you think?'

Big Jim showed Parkins a grin, then put it away and went over to where French Henry lay, a safe distance from anything that might have tumbled toward him from the blast. He sank to a knee, seeing how grey Henry's face was. His eyes were open but Jim Deal wasn't sure what he was seeing. He'd seen similar expressions on other men's faces when they were close to death, and he'd often wondered about it, if it wasn't a sign they were glimpsing the great beyond already, to wherever it was in heaven men like Big Jim and those others who broke the law and took lives went to upon shuffling off their mortal coils.

'Hey Henry,' he said gently.

The man's eyes focused on Jim, recognized him. His lips moved.

'What's that?' Big Jim leaned closer, putting his ear to the man's face.

'The Quiet One,' French Henry managed to whisper.

'Yeah, what about him?' Jim wouldn't call it a premonition, but he had an idea he was about to hear something he didn't want to hear.

'Will, he's called. Will Tayling.'

'Uh huh. That's the name he signed on with us as. What about him, Henry? He's away off with Kline and Finn, tackling the train in case you couldn't do the charges. But we sorted that one out. You don't need to worry about the Quiet One. You did good.'

'But you need to worry 'bout him, boss. I remember where I seen him before. He's a Ranger, Jim. He was younger back then, but he's one of the guys took me in for blastin' that armoured stage and stealin' the money in Texas. Only just starting to wear his hat like he does, but you could see it in him, the man he'd become. He's the same guy. Will Tayling, Texas Ranger. Don't trust him.'

With that, the last of French Henry's life left him. His body sagged, a lifeless husk.

Big Jim waited, fuming. Waited until he was sure the train wasn't coming. After building a small cairn for French Henry, the least the man deserved, the gang tracked back along the railroad. Eventually they came upon a burned body. They couldn't tell whose it was. A little further down the line, they found another corpse. Its face was punched in, and the back of the head missing. There wasn't any sign of the train.

Jack Kilkenny said, 'Maybe they went back, including this Ranger fella been hiding amongst us, and the artist too. The Wolf's safe if that's the case, until they try again.'

Big Jim strode around, leaving his horse to stringy Pete Kingsley to look after while he tried to see what had gone down. There was a spattering of water, still not dried on the sleepers, from where the train had stopped. If any railroad men had been killed in the raid, their bodies had been recovered and were no doubt travelling east along with the rest of the passengers. There *were* a couple of trails in the grass, not very distinct it was true, made as if whoever had put them down had done their best to leave no sign they'd ever been that way.

'Two horses heading that way, aiming to take the long route around the hills to Autumn Jericho,' Big Jim said. 'I was to lay a bet, I'd say they're Mister Will Tayling's, aka the Quiet One, aka our Ranger lawman. He's trying to get that artist fella to town.'

When he looked through his spyglass, he couldn't see them. But he'd an idea which route they'd taken. They'd never make it. He vowed that beneath a sky as blue as the Lord knew how to make them. No sir, if Big Jim Deal had any influence on the world – Big Jim who commanded thunder and brought mountains crashing down – then Will 'the Quiet One' Tayling and whatever sorry-assed sob he was herding along to Autumn Jericho to get out pencil and paper wouldn't ever get to their destination.

Will had to hand it to her, the girl could ride. She followed the trail he'd put her on without much trouble, letting the horse find its feet as it climbed the steep slope through the trees and then, once they'd peaked near the summit, down into the valley beyond. When the branches of the trees hung low, she ducked and suffered leaves through her hair and in her face without complaint, though it was beginning to tell on her. She finally allowed Will to take the lead only when they came to a stream, their horses kicking up glints of water that shone like diamonds in the sun. Once they'd crossed, Will called them to a stop.

She said, 'How'm I doing? Keeping ahead of your ugly friends?'

'I reckon we're still in front of them.'

'How's it you're so sure they'll come after us?'

'Because they need to. Because their pride will hurt after what happened back on the train. And because you're a danger to them. You get to Autumn Jericho, sketch up a good likeness of the Black Wolf, then his face is known. Someone'll recognize him and he'll be caught, hanged most likely. Jim and his men won't last long on their own.'

Sam hadn't considered the ultimate ramifications of what she'd be doing in Autumn Jericho. A man's life depended on her skill with a pencil. But then, she supposed, plenty more than just one man's did. Though the Black Wolf might forfeit his life after she'd drawn him up, plenty of others would be saved from him.

'What're you doing now?' she asked as Will slid off his mount.

He pulled skin-covered canteens from the saddle of his own horse and then hers as well. 'Replenishing supplies. Get off and allow your animal to drink, graze if he's a mind.'

Sam did as Will instructed, carefully preserving her modesty by holding her skirt as she came off, impressing Will with her dexterity as well as her poise. She'd impressed him back on the train too, clobbering Anders Finn and in the process saving Will a bullet wound and very possibly his life too.

She'd also talked one of her fellow passengers on to the roof of the train to provide the rifle shot that had given him time to fight back on the steam plate. She was a game one, stuck things out. Will always warmed to folk like that.

'What's funny?' she asked him.

'Nothing.'

'Then why're you smiling?'

'Didn't realize I was. Or that it needed remarking upon.'

'Mister Tayling, when you smile I don't know if I should be happy or just afraid.'

When Will had filled up their canteens he checked the animals to see they'd made it over the harsher trails without injury. He was anxious to keep travelling, and Sam supposed the bad men he'd told her about, led by this Big Jim Deal character, must be every bit as mean and dangerous as the bandits who'd attacked the train. Maybe more so.

Given the circumstances, Sam did not wish to make the acquaintance of these men. So when Will said they should go, she did not argue or complain that her lower back was stiff, and getting all the more sore because of the box with her artist's materials inside. Nor did she complain that her jacket was now so torn it snagged on every twisty branch and thorn in her way. Instead, she nodded and raised herself up on the stirrups and followed his lead, going after his horse with her own, leaving the peaceful and calming music of the stream behind.

She felt calm, despite the hardships before her. Her only wish was that she'd time to stop and sketch, because the landscape around them was stunning. All these trees stacked one on top of the other, climbing the hillsides, the peaks of the mountains in the distance.

Perhaps she'd have felt differently if she'd had a mind to look behind her. But she didn't. And so neither she nor Will saw a glint of light from high up in the hills they'd descended. The reflection of the sun striking the magnifying lens of a spyglass.

CHAPTER 8

Gus had heard nothing but good things about Landon Coyle, the preacher and Sunday school teacher. Now he'd spent more time with him, his impression was that for all the surface calm and respectability he gave off – a man who at first glance was entirely at peace with his place in God's creation – there was beneath it all a troubling rash of nervousness.

'I'm so sorry about all of this,' Landon Coyle said. He'd removed his wide-brimmed hat, revealing sandy-coloured hair as smooth as silk. 'How terrible for you.'

He was talking to the Widow Leigh, clasping her hands inside both of his. He had long, slim hands that were nicely browned, the way the loaves Molly Haskin passed to you at the counter of the dry goods store in town were; a sign he spent a good deal of time outdoors, where he'd been known to preach, standing on the back of a buck wagon and saying it

89

was more than the Lord God Jesus Christ had to preach out of in his time, so it was more than plenty for lowly Landon Coyle. A preacher with a sense of his own inconsequentialities, Will Tayling had once said to Gus as the pair had passed by his preaching truck one time. Gus was never entirely sure if Will was joking or not.

'It's all so much to deal with,' Karen Leigh said, as if she were unburdening herself, soul and all, of her troubles to the man.

Landon Coyle frowned sympathetically. 'And the little girl. Tara?'

'Tara-May.'

'Yes, of course. How is she?'

'Sheriff Dudgeon's wife's looking over her, insists she rests while we get ready.'

'Then right now wouldn't be an appropriate time for me to have our little chat about ghosts and how she's no need to be fearful of her dreams?'

Gus intervened. 'We don't have time for that.' If his rifle, and the way he stood warily beside the door, one eye glancing out every few seconds to be sure they were safe wasn't the clue, then he didn't know what was. 'We're riding into town the second we get a chance. Before the Black Wolf rounds up more men and sends them over here.'

'The Black Wolf?' The preacher appeared visibly shaken. 'You're sure it's him?'

'No one else with reason to come shooting up after Missus Leigh and Tara-May.'

'Then your plan is. . . ?'

'We're hitching into Autumn Jericho. Safest four walls in town are my offices in the jailhouse. We'll run on in there, soon as my deputy fixes up some horses to a buggy.'

'But you can't stay there indefinitely.'

'Hoping there won't be a need to. Got us a portrait artist due on the train. Soon as he's arrived, I'm gonna escort him to the jailhouse, let him draw up a likeness of the Black Wolf. We'll see what he looks like. Won't be able to hide then; someone'll recognize him.'

The preacher's face, for all its rich tan, paled. He put a hand to his dog collar. 'My.'

'But Mister Coyle can come with us, can't he?' Karen Leigh said. 'I'm sure it'll help Tara-May if he's there. She'll be more relaxed if he can reassure her everything's all right.'

Gus thought on how the little girl had stood in the doorway, looking lost and forlorn in the wake of all the bullets, the smell of cordite still hanging in the air, and how she'd said, 'Ain't nowhere safe.'

'Sure,' he said. 'Be right useful having you along, Preacher.'

The buggy bumped along the trail. Gus urged the horses on as fast as he dared. When he was a younger man, along with his friend Will Tayling, he'd raced carts and horses for fun. Now he was fast relearning that old skill, and pushing it to the max. They had to

91

get to Autumn Jericho before any of the Black Wolf's men could descend on them.

'Must we go so fast?' Mainey said, reaching from the back and clutching his arm.

'Ain't no choice. We go any slower, we risk being picked off by anyone with a good enough aim. Duck back down there, honey.'

She sank into the bed of the buggy, where a frightened Karen Leigh did her best not to show her fears to her daughter. The girl was huddled between Karen and Mainey. Sitting alongside Gus, Landon Coyle uncomfortably held on to Gus's rifle, while one hand gripped the edge of his seat to prevent himself tumbling off. He'd left his own horse in the Dudgeons' fenced-in corral, knowing he wouldn't be able to keep up all the way to Autumn Jericho.

'We're getting there,' Coyle called to the ladies, though Gus had to smile on hearing his voice. The preacher sounded as if he might bring up his breakfast.

It was one of the few smiles Gus allowed himself along the trail. For the most part he was concentrating hard, making sure to keep an eye out for the best route to ride the buggy along, wary of any surprise attack the Black Wolf might throw at them.

'Yee-haw!' he heard Taylor Quinn shout out up ahead, head ducked low beside his horse's. Behind the buggy, bringing up the rear in case of an attack from behind, and sometimes running up alongside the buggy, at Gus's side one minute, and then at the preacher's the next, Ethan Hague kept pace with them. Both deputies had their eyes peeled for danger. As it was, when the attack came, it both arrived on them by surprise and was over almost before it had begun.

Shots rang out and hit the wooden slats on the preacher's side of the buggy, right behind the riding seat. They sent splinters into the air, which flew back and out of the way like long stalks of hay caught in a tornado. Another bullet whistled in, pinged on a metal bolt (springing it free with enough momentum it could've easily killed someone had it not shot harmlessly into the woods on the other side of the buggy) and whined away into the distance.

Screams came from in back of the truck and for a moment Gus thought one of the women had been hit. But they were screams of fear, not pain.

'Faster!' Landon Coyle shouted, and made a ham-fisted job out of raising the rifle at whoever was taking the shots, trying to find where his finger should go to pull on the trigger.

Gus was running the rig as fast as he could – beyond, he was afraid to admit, his own skill levels. They'd been lucky so far, avoiding obstacles in their course as much by good fortune than because of any driving ability he was displaying. His reflexes weren't what they had been as a young man. But he'd expected trouble along the way. Now they were getting it.

'Where they shooting from?' he asked, lashing the

horses and sending a prayer up through his gritted teeth to whatever God might hear it.

'From the side of the hill there.'

'Shoot back. Just point and press the trigger. You don't have to hit them.'

They passed Taylor Quinn as he slowed to aim and shoot. Gus yelled, feeling his words snatched from his mouth by the speed of the buggy's passage, 'Leave them alone, concentrate on getting into town safely!' He glanced over his shoulder to see Quinn pick up the pace. 'Shoot while you're riding, makes for a harder target!' Ethan Hague was already doing so, despite his injured hand. Beside Gus, Landon Coyle didn't seem to know one end of his rifle from the other. There wasn't going to be much covering fire from that direction. Then from in back of the buggy, Mainey cried, 'Look, it's him. The Wolf!'

'Get your head down,' Gus ordered, his first instinct to keep his wife safe.

'But look, Gus – my Lord, it's him!'

Gus had to look where she was pointing, if only to satisfy his curiosity. There, sure enough, mounted on a pitch-black horse well beyond shooting range, was the Black Wolf. A figure cut of cloth as dark as the night: caped, tall, in the strangest mask Gus Dudgeon had ever seen a criminal wear in his years as a lawman. As his wolves ran forward, men in garb as dark as his own, preparing to shoot again, Gus saw the Black Wolf raise an arm, probably calling the men back, voice emerging from out of that gaping maw filled with sharp teeth.

But why? They could get lucky with a long-range shot, take out Tara-May, and all the Wolf's worries would be over.

As the buggy sped into the cover of thick trees forming a tunnel overhead, Gus saw the Black Wolf raise his hands again as if aiming a rifle, then mime shooting. He did it deliberately and with great care. But not a single shot followed.

'The hell?' Gus said, and shook his head, not caring any more. With Quinn and Hague running alongside the buggy again, Gus set his attention on the road, rattling over old wagon tracks and places where the mud had dried out to form hard ruts. It wasn't an easy ride, but from there on in it was as safe a ride as they could've hoped for.

All the same, Gus's heart didn't stop pounding all the way into Autumn Jericho, not even when they'd run at a dangerous pace along the outer edges of the built up area, passing clapboard houses and log cabins, and banked a hard right on to Main Street, hurtling by the stores and saloon, and skidded to a stop in front of the jailhouse, the wagon all but collapsing.

Will had warned her that the going wouldn't be easy. But she'd told him she could handle it. Hadn't she ridden when she was a child? She hadn't been on the back of a horse in many a year now, but it wasn't a skill you lost. All the same, dressed up like this, it was hard work.

As the trail narrowed, Sam cussed as her blouse caught and tore, exposing a length of flesh on her upper arm. Her jacket had been ripped to shreds, so she'd taken that off, had lost it somewhere along the way. Now she'd to rein back the horse to untangle herself. She didn't know what kind of tree had snagged her, but it had hooky little twigs that were a swine to escape once they'd caught. There were plenty more of the trees crowding in on her ahead.

'This's happened too many times,' Will Tayling told her from beneath the brim of his hat. He was watching her over one shoulder. She could tell he was impatient to press on.

'Well, I didn't set out on this journey thinking I'd be crossing the wilds on the back of a horse,' Sam retorted, frustrated and tired, and yes, darn sore where the hard edge of her illustrator's box was rubbing away at her lower back.

'Maybe, ma'am—'

'And will you stop calling me "ma'am". My name's Samantha Sloane. Call me Sam if you have to call me anything.'

Will stayed quiet as she tried to unsnag herself from the tree while maintaining the integrity of her blouse. All she did, however, was worsen the rip, leaving the sleeve split the length of its seam.

'Sam,' Will Tayling said.

'What now?' she almost spat.

'I can see you're troubled, upset and tired, likely,

but we need to press on. It's a sure bet that Big Jim's gonna be following us. It won't take him and his men long to catch up if we have to keep stopping like this. And it's not like we're moving at a fast trot as it is.'

Sam knew that every word he spoke was the truth. She hated herself all the more for it, hated to sound like she was begging, but she said, 'Can you help me here?'

Will nodded but didn't move. 'If I'm gonna be calling you Sam, it's only right you call me by my name too.'

It took a moment, but she said, 'Will. I'd be obliged if you could help me. Please.'

When she was free, rubbing down her arm, where scratches had appeared as if she'd been handling an uppity tomcat, Will told her to step off her horse. She did as he instructed; there was no disguising how tired she was. Whereas before she'd dismounted with an eye to maintaining her modesty when she lifted her legs over the saddle – Will had at first been surprised to see her ride like a man and not attempt to side-saddle – she now just let herself flop off the horse, not caring she was exposing her underskirt as she came down.

'Stand here in front of me,' Will told her.

Duly obeying, she flounced over to him, shoulders sagging. She was breathing heavily, verging on tears.

'It's all right.' He hunted soothing words. 'We'll be over the worst of it by nightfall.'

'You mean, we won't be in Autumn Jericho before it's dark?'

97

'Sam, we won't be in Autumn Jericho until the middle of tomorrow at best.'

'We have to sleep out here? Under the sky?'

'Only if Big Jim and his men don't catch up on us,' he said. 'If they do . . . well, we might be sleeping sooner than that, and for ever. Which means we can't go leaving them strips of cloth to track us by. Any darn fool who's never left a city could follow the trail we've been laying. It's as good as signposted for them. I'd hoped we'd be quick enough it wouldn't matter, but we're not.'

'So what're you proposing?'

'This.' Will tugged a wicked-looking knife from the back of his boot. It was curved, glinting with a shine that could cut a hair in half, and had scythed teeth on its inner curl.

She didn't object. Knew she had to endure this, that he was right. What she was wearing just wasn't practical. So standing upright, watched on by the horses, and with as much dignity as she could manage, Sam let Will Tayling go to work on her clothing, as no man had ever been to work on her before, slicing off strips of cotton left, right, and centre. They fell to the ground around her in long curls.

When he was finished with her clothes, he put a hand up to the back of her hair, and she cried, 'Hey, no!'

He paused, holding on to her, not saying a word.

'Do we have to?' Her hair, for goodness' sake. She

98

didn't want to lose her hair.

'S'for the best.'

She closed her eyes, acquiescing. It was all she could do not to weep when she felt the tug at the back of her head and then the lightness afterward as her hair fell around her.

When he'd done, she turned away, unable to look him in the eye. She put her hand to feel what he'd done to her, thinking she must look like a boy who lived in the wildwoods.

Will slid the knife back in the sheaf tucked into the back of his left boot, then caught hold of his horse and swung himself aboard. 'You coming?' he asked her.

She took a moment to compose herself, stepped over the strips of her clothes, and not caring for a moment how much of her leg she showed, pulled herself up on to her own mount. He'd taken her artist's box and carried it himself now; she was grateful for that. As they rode on, pressing deeper into the thick woods, she didn't much care now about the low hanging branches and how much the trees pressed in on her. She pushed through with barely a hitch.

They moved faster. But it still wasn't fast enough.

CHAPTER 9

The sheriff's office and jailhouse seemed to shun the light, as if it was a hostile force it was aiming to repel. Right now, Gus Dudgeon was more than happy to be experiencing that feeling of solidity and protection the building's thick walls offered up.

Soon as they'd arrived, hustling Tara-May inside, along with her ma and hot on their heels his own good wife, Mainey Jessica Dudgeon, Gus had back-tracked to the door, eyes looking for danger along the length of Main Street, until he pulled that heavy oak wood closed and not only twisted the big old iron key in the lock but slid in the bolts and slammed the extra security of the iron drop bar in place too.

'The shoot's going on?' Leo Enwright spoke up as the group shut up the jailhouse. 'Sheriff? Ethan?'

Ignoring him, Gus paced to the back of the building, where a twin set of barred cells took up the wall space. A figure lounged on a wooden pallet bed, shadowed in the darkness. He pushed himself up.

Recognizing Garth Brady, Gus said to Enwright, 'Cut him loose.'

'I hear you right?'

'Let him out, Leo.'

Enwright squinted out of his better eye at his boss. 'You sure you ain't ill, Sheriff? You told Brady here, any more of that drunkenness at Paige's saloon and you'd keep him in a week. Ethan Hague, he only done clanged the cell door shut on him last night.'

Leo looked to Ethan for confirmation, only to see the deputy pulling the shutters in on the windows, further darkening the already gloomy jailhouse.

'Well, shoot me,' Leo said, finally getting that something big was going down. That little girl the sheriff had brought in surely didn't look happy, nor did her mother, standing tense and lost alongside Gus Dudgeon's wife. Even the preacher man, Landon Coyle – Leo had seen him giving a sermon and had to admit the man knew his Bible – was here, looking pale and uncomfortable holding on to a big Winchester rifle like it was a rattlesnake.

'Open the cell, kick him out, and be mindful to lock that door after him,' Gus said as Leo scuttled to the wall to unhook the cell keys.

Gus made for the lower drawer of his desk and pulled out boxes of ammunition, started filling up a spare pistol in a holster, which he tied down on his left leg, thereby matching the weapon on his right.

'Sheriff,' Landon Coyle said, and Gus looked his way as if he'd forgotten all about him.

101

'You did all right, back there,' Gus told him, even though he didn't believe the preacher had fired a shot at the Black Wolf and his men.

'Well, I don't know about that,' Coyle said, moving back awkwardly to let Leo Enwright escort a clearly hungover Garth Brady past him. Enwright muttered to himself about locks and keys and the place being as solid as a bank vault while he opened the door, nodded to Deputy Taylor Quinn outside, who'd positioned himself behind an upright beam holding the porch roof up, and pushed Brady out and down the steps to the dusty hard pan.

'Leo,' Quinn said, greeting the old-timer with a nod.

Nodding back, Leo tugged the white of his beard, and crabbed back inside, really not liking the way Quinn's gaze was as hard as steel as he scanned the streets and walks.

Inside, with the door locked and bolted and the iron bar back in place, Leo sought the Sheriff's ear, only to find him still talking to the preacher. 'I can understand you'd be worried about the Black Wolf seeing you with us, especially after what became of Patch Amory. But I'm sure he knows you're a preacher, not a portrait artist. I don't see no reason for you to stay with us. You've seen the dangers in being with us. You're welcome to go if you want.'

Before Leo Enwright could finally demand to know what the cotton-picking blazes was going on, the young woman he took to be the child's mother came forward, all but wrapping herself around the preacher's arm. He was a man of God and all, but Leo wouldn't have blamed him for that quick-fire look of desire that flickered across his face, having a good-looking woman like that fawn over him, so needy and all.

'No, please don't go, Mister Coyle,' she urged. 'Stay. He can stay, can't he, Sheriff?'

'Now, ma'am, the Black Wolf will know where we are. I'm not of a mind to risk more lives than I need to. And if there's any way I can move you and my wife out, just keep Tara-May safely inside the jailhouse, then what's what I'd be tempted to do.'

'I'm not leaving my daughter.'

'Right now I don't have anywhere to send you to, so it's no concern. Mister Coyle, however, I'm sure there's plenty of places he'll be fine at.'

'But Mister Coyle would help. Don't you see? Tara-May would be a better witness if she wasn't so scared. Mister Coyle can help with her dreams. She'll be easier having someone like him about the place. That's why he came back with us after all.'

Coyle, stammering slightly, and no doubt thinking of being some place the Black Wolf might take a shot at him, nodded. 'I do believe I might be able to calm the child, Sheriff. Ghosts and fear of ghosts, that is my line of work, albeit in an indirect way.'

Letting go of the preacher and leaning over to plant her hands on Gus's desk, Karen Leigh said, 'Have him stay with us. Please.'

Hearing the door locked and bolted behind him, Gus stood up straight, confident Ethan Hague could look after things. Leo Enwright was beside Gus, the town jailer in his best pants and braces, a man rumoured to be closing in on a hundred years old by the town's children, but actually just topping up on over sixty. 'Walk with you, Sheriff?' he said now.

'That'd be grand, Leo. Make it look like we're doing a little patrol of the town.'

'Garth Brady knows what's going on in the jail.'

'Naw, he's too hungover to remember anything. In fact, I'd lay ten bits that he's looking to score another drink right now, ain't thinking nothing at all beyond that.' Gus turned to Taylor Quinn, who'd acquitted himself very handily throughout the day's events so far. 'Taylor, gonna saunter on up the street, take a look at anyone coming in on the railroad.'

'Train's past due,' Quinn said, understanding what the sheriff was really saying.

'That it is, Deputy Quinn,' Gus said, nodding politely at two colourful ladies crossing the street. He touched his fingers to the tip of his hat. 'That it is. Let's take that walk, Leo. And Taylor, you keep an eye on things here.'

Gus Dudgeon, hat straight on his head, a couple of gun-belts around his waist, stepped off the wooden porch fronting the jailhouse, Leo beside him, and crossed to the wooden walk leading down Main

Street. Doing it casually, but feeling a need to get to the station, because it was Gus Dudgeon's sincere belief that if he could get his special passenger off that train and into the safety of the jailhouse as soon as was humanly possible, then all of this would quickly be over for the poor little girl and her ma. With a likeness, he and the rest of the law enforcement officials across the state could get to work running down the Black Wolf.

'Sheriff, why're we doing this?' Leo said, sensible enough to ask his question when no one might overhear.

'Sorry to have kept you out of the picture so long, Leo. There's someone coming in on the train, should be able to draw up a portrait of the Black Wolf with that little girl's help.' Gus told him about the fire at the Leigh household, how the Black Wolf's men had tracked them to Gus's place, the ambush that wasn't quite an ambush on the route into town.

'Mighty strange he didn't shoot at you more,' Leo said.

'Been pondering on that myself.'

They carried on along the walk, tipping hats at the ladies out on the boards, and being careful not to linger making smalltalk. They passed the post office and the general store – where Mitch Cullin was attempting his hand at signwriting on the window. 'Only two Ts in potato,' Leo told him as they passed by, raising a smile from Gus and about a hundred cusses from Mitch – and then on by the smithy toward Paige Somerfield's saloon.

They were walking by when a sassy voice called, 'Hey, Sheriff. Where you been?'

'Careful there, Sheriff,' Leo warned as Gus pulled up, 'you don't want to be getting into trouble with Mainey, now do you?'

'That was a different time and a different place, Leo.'

'I'm only saying, that's all.'

'Sure you are.' Gus nodded. 'Wander on up to the station, see if you can't find a buggy and a horse or two. Mine's done for. I'll catch up with you.'

As Leo walked off, his legs bandy and splayed but still game enough to carry him along at a good hop, Gus Dudgeon turned to the smiling woman who, with very much up front in all sorts of ways, now stood hanging on to the swing doors of her saloon.

'Tempt you, Sheriff?'

'Always nice to see you, Paige.'

'Your wife think the same?'

'Anyone ever tell you you've got a wicked grin on you?'

'I think that maybe they did, and that maybe the person who told me that's standing right in front of me.' She raised an eyebrow. 'Fully loaded too, I see.'

Gus instinctively fingered his pistol grips. Paige's face went dark and serious. 'What's wrong, Gus?'

He sighed. 'I can trust you, can't I, Paige?'

She nodded slowly. If there was any ambiguity in it, he didn't see it. 'To a point.'

He told her as much as he thought safe to, finishing with, 'There's something I'm not seeing. An informer for the Black Wolf, Paige. Someone in town seems to know everything I do as soon as I do it, if not before. You hear anything?'

She shook her head, coming out of the doorway to stand before him. Couldn't help it, she raised her fingers to his badge, lingering on the points of the star. 'I'd tell you anything I could that'd help, you know that.'

'I guess I do.'

'If it's not someone you trust, who's right close to you, then it's got to be someone else, the little girl's side of things, or the missing boy's family. You all kept them in the loop about how things were going, didn't you?'

She had a point. He'd told Bucky Wright's parents everything. And it was straight after visiting them that his own home had been attacked. All the same, good a fit as it was, Gus found it hard to understand why they'd inform on Tara-May's whereabouts to the Black Wolf, unless one of them, the husband say, was a member of one of his gangs. It was possible. The Wolf commanded high loyalty among his men, the so-called wolves.

'Much obliged, Paige,' Gus said, noticing the hands of the town clock had inched closer to half past two, already thirty minutes after the train was due in. 'You've given me something to think on.'

'You're welcome, Sheriff,' she said, going all sassy

again. 'You be sure to come back whenever you need me. I'll be waiting.'

The train didn't come and the train didn't come. Gus was finding it hard to contain his patience. He watched the railroad people preparing for its arrival. Fuel was set to dump in the coal truck, the water tower's hose ready to be levered out on to the loco-motive engine. But no matter how hard he peered down the track, there was no sign among the flicker-ing heat-snakes of that big old cattle-ram on the front of the engine.

'Something ain't right,' he whispered when fifteen minutes of waiting threatened to stretch to thirty. The train was over forty-five minutes late.

The other people on the platform, there for friends and loved ones or maybe for the mail and supplies, were beginning to leave. Leo Enwright questioned Stevie Warne, who acted as sometime sta-tionmaster, and it looked like he didn't have a mind to know what was going on either. Leo shook his head at Gus, letting him know there was no news.

'It seems the train's been delayed,' a rich voice said beside Gus.

Turning to see who'd spoken, Gus couldn't help but stand a little straighter, stiffening. 'Mister Masters,' he said. 'You expecting people on the train?'

Hugh Masters smiled. Although he was a foppish sort, and often pressed his nose into a scented hand-kerchief, he was a tall man. He had influence not only in Autumn Jericho but the surrounding areas too. He was known to be wealthy, served as a town alderman, and his donations to good causes and the upkeep of the churches had not gone unnoticed. 'I had hoped to see someone in,' he said. 'Now it seems that the effort's been for nothing.'

'Well, maybe it'll come later,' Gus said, but he knew something had happened to the train. It wouldn't be this long overdue unless it'd come to some mishap. Will, he thought, I hope if you've had any part in this that you've done your job well and kept that artist safe.

He peered down the line again, but it was as empty as before.

'. . . Would you say?'

'Sorry, what's that?' Gus said, when he realized Hugh Masters was speaking, the tall man dressed in a combination of grey silk vest and black trousers today.

'I said, I hope you'll tell me if it's inconvenient, but I do understand from the streets – a man can't help hearing the gossip, you know – that there's a bit of trouble in town. After everything we discussed at the last meeting of the aldermen, about your plan to capture the Black Wolf, if it's easier for you to have your good lady wife somewhere safe tonight, I'm sure I can arrange something. . . .'

'That's very kind of you, Mister Masters,' Gus said. 'That would help solve a lot of my worries but I'm a bit busy to be sure of escorting her to your place.'

109

Especially if there's no artist arriving today and I have to protect that child for another night, Gus thought, praying that no more information was getting out to his enemy. . . .

Then it struck him. Paige Somerfield had been right. There was someone close to the Leigh family who'd access to all the news, knew exactly what was going on. It wasn't just Bucky Wright's family, after all. Gus turned from Hugh Masters and ran, shouting at Leo to wait and see if the train arrived, while he sprinted from the station, hoping and praying – if there wasn't any irony or cruel mockery in that action – that the little girl was all right and that Ethan Hague's injured hand didn't have him at a severe disadvantage right now.

When he'd pointedly mimed that shooting gesture, the Black Wolf hadn't been mocking or threatening them. He'd been sending a message. *Do as I say. Shoot the witness.*

Passing that message on to the preacher, Landon Coyle, who'd been called in a day before the Leigh house got burned down to exorcise the ghosts of Tara-May's dream memories. Coyle. The informer.

They rode quickly and they rode relentlessly. Big Jim Deal's gang moved like the cohorts of the Black Wolf that they were. Swiftly, like dark beasts flowing over the landscape with stealth and certainty, following the trail that the Quiet One and the portrait artist had left. And then they'd spotted them. At the bottom of the valley, taking a break to refill their water. Will Tayling, the betrayer, and the portrait artist himself.

Only, Big Jim realized, when he'd sighted his spyglass on them and extended it to its full range, the portrait artist wasn't no man at all. 'I'll be. . . .' he said and laughed.

Parkins Whelks looked up at his boss. 'What's so funny?'

'Our man, the portrait artist we were looking for. Well, I gotta hand it to them, that was smart. He ain't a man at all. They brought a woman in to do the job.'

Big Jim laughed again. Jack Kilkenny rode over to the pair of them, leaving Spinny Ben and Rush Auster together with John Beale and Ken Lovell. Kilkenny had his long-barrelled rifle with him, shooting sight aimed in the air. 'Hey boss, you want me to take a shot? I could wing one of them, maybe worse, with a bit of luck.'

'Not from here. You miss and it'll just encourage them to ride all the faster. Mister Quiet One Will Tayling may not even know we're following him. Probably thinks he's outsmarted us and we're still waiting back at the cut for the train. I'd like to see what he has to say for himself when we meet up. And I've a mind or two things to say to that gal he's got riding with him too. Happen she'd like to draw me at some point.'

They tracked Will Tayling the rest of the afternoon, following snagged threads of clothing, eventually coming upon a spot where a spread of shredded cotton lay breezing around a small clearing along a narrow trail where the trees crowded in and the branches hung low and tough couch grass tugged at their mounts' feet.

'What do you think happened?' Parkins Whelks asked. 'He do something to her?'

'Cut down her clothes,' Big Jim said, seeing it in his mind's eye. 'She was getting snagged up in the woods. Wasn't suited for being out here in the country. Was expecting to ride into Jericho on the train.'

'This must've come as a shock to her then,' Parkins said.

'Ain't nothing to the shock she's gonna get when we catch up on her.'

After that, though the trail wasn't so obvious now that occasional threads of tweed or cotton weren't there to follow, they wound around the valley floor, criss-crossing the stream twice, rarely taking the opportunity to give their horses a rest. Big Jim was determined to catch up with Tayling, see to it that he never got to say he'd outsmarted Big Jim Deal.

'I'm pretty sure they're following us,' Will said.

Sam hadn't realized he'd gone back to take a look. She'd simply been holding on to her horse, letting it find its own way along the faint trail Will had pointed her down, expecting he'd just decided to ride behind her for a while. She was lulled half asleep by the sun and the dappled shadows here in the vast woods, by the heat of late summer. Even the pesky insects buzzing in to take a bite out of her no longer bothered her, she simply endured them as she had endured the cuts and scrapes on her exposed flesh, the indignity of Will Tayling cutting her clothes down to next to nothing. She shook her head to rouse herself. 'How far behind are they?'

'Not far enough. We should've put all the bodies on board the train, not just the guards and the conductor. The bodies showed where we set off from, pointed them our way. My mistake.' Will chewed on his jaw. 'We push on, try move faster.'

In time, with the sun sinking behind the mountains and the first shadows of night pressing forth, they came upon the abandoned cabin.

CHAPTER 10

Tara-May Leigh hadn't said much since the bad men had shot up the sheriff's house that morning. She'd meekly gone about lying down in the back of the dusty old buggy and jumped and rattled like a pea in a can as she and her ma had been raced along faster than Tara-May ever thought she'd ridden in her life. True, she'd screamed when the gunshots sounded and the safe haven in back of the buggy – which in truth hadn't seemed all that safe to begin with, and more like an accident waiting to happen – was torn up into splinters.

But that was the only noise she'd made. While everyone else had turned to look at the Black Wolf, she'd sunk down lower, never wanting to see the frightening wolf mask again.

And now here she was in the jailhouse with her ma and the sheriff's nice wife, and she was hearing that jingling noise again, the one she remembered – and which cut through her dreams, turning them into nightmares – from that night she saw the Black Wolf.

Fearfully, Tara-May looked around from where she was laying on the cot. It was darker here in the cell. The shadows didn't so much seem to hug the wall as live there, building a whole other world to get lost within. But it wasn't a world she wanted to enter. Prowling, slinking things might live in it. Things like Bucky's ghost and the Black Wolf and the secret face he kept hidden from this world.

Her ma had left her on the cot, to go fetch some water from the pail by the pot-bellied woodstove. Because the jailhouse windows were so mean, even crueller with the shutters being put across the glass, the only illumination came from lantern light and a couple of candles standing up in their own wax.

Now, as people moved around, the candles guttered and swayed, like dancing imps or fairies or whatever spirits the Indians claimed lived within the endless forests. As they dipped and danced and swayed, the shadows of people crept long and thin or bunched into squatting pygmies around the walls. And still that jingling kept making its noise.

Tara-May turned very slowly in her cot, looking to the open door of the cell, and lit on the source of that sound. A shiver spread up the ridges of her spine, like a dead man's hand walking fingers cold from the grave right on up it.

She recognized the shoes from that night she'd spent cowering in the undergrowth, the same little repaired seam that you could only see if you really knew to look for it by the right knee. When she looked up and found him staring at her, she could see in his eyes that he'd realized she knew the truth of him.

He stopped jangling the cruciform that had given him away. He let it fall on its chain and gripped the rifle he held with both hands.

Still in shape for all that he was approaching his forty-fifth year, Gus Dudgeon raced down the wooden ramp from the station platform, ignoring Enwright's questioning yells. Leo had fixed up a wagon to transport the portrait artist, as Gus had asked him to. He'd pointed it out when Gus had arrived at the station after his chat with Paige Somerfield (a chat Leo Enwright was smart enough not to jibe Gus about). It was to this horse and wagon that Gus ran. He climbed on board, kicked off the brake and spat, 'Yah! Yah! Yah!' to get the horse to move.

Exactly what the Black Wolf had promised Landon Coyle, Gus didn't know. Maybe a church of his own, no more running around preaching out the back of a bust-up old wagon. But Gus was willing to bet any riches the preacher received from the Wolf were no incentive compared to the threats he could issue – and no doubt follow up on.

Darn it, but didn't that explain so much. The Black Wolf had told his men to stop firing on the buggy for fear they'd hit their inside man and miss the child completely. The Wolf had made sure to issue his command to the preacher with that mime he'd made.

Shoot the witness. Make sure of it.

Belting along the road and rounding on to Main Street, the horse whinnied and neighed, protesting at the cracks Gus was applying through the reins. The wagon wheels lifted off the ground on one side, the whole threatening to tip over, but Gus kept control. He stood up on the running board, shouting at folks to clear the way, which they duly did, scattering as he ploughed on like a crazy man. He rounded a slowing stage and folks dived to the walkways to make way for him as he kicked up dust, aiming for the jailhouse.

Taylor Quinn came to the front of the porch, rifle in hand, wondering what the danger was as Gus slowed to a stop, nearly tipping over in his haste to get there in time. 'The hail, Sheriff? What's going on? Where's Leo? Is he all right?'

Gus tumbled off the cart, hit the dirt, scrambling to his feet and making for the jailhouse door, even as a bewildered Taylor Quinn looked around seeking trouble or an explanation and the skittered horse clomped off, dragging the wagon after it. But Gus hadn't time for words, was pulling a Colt out as he leaped up the three old bowed steps to the porch, pressing ahead for the jailhouse door . . . finding it locked.

*

The sudden banging on the door made everyone jump. Tara-May all but yelped, and Landon Coyle – standing sweating at the entrance to the cell – he twitched too.

'It's me, let me in.'

'Sheriff?' Ethan Hague pushed back his seat and excused himself from Mainey's ministrations. She'd been trying to bandage his hand while leaving enough flexibility in his fingers for him to work his gun. He went to the door, leaving his pistol on the table.

'Deputy Hague,' Tara-May's ma said, 'didn't the sheriff say to only admit someone if they were to tap on the door in a special way?'

'Thank you, ma'am, he did,' Ethan Hague acknowledged, cradling his awkward hand as he went to the door. He leaned against it, only half-smiling, thinking his boss sounded pretty serious. 'Hey Gus, you know what you told us about knocking on this door.'

'Say what? Just open the damn door, Ethan.'

'Well, all right,' Ethan said, turning back to flash a grin at Tara-May's ma. He was about to lift his good hand up to slide back the bolts, but he was called down by the preacher. 'Deputy Hague. Please don't open the door.'

Ethan Hague's expression would've been funny in another situation. But not with Landon Coyle taking firm stock of the rifle he held, and with none of the butter-fingered skill he'd displayed riding in on the buggy, levelling it at the deputy in a way that said he knew how to use the weapon.

'It's him,' Tara-May spoke up from her cot, the blanket pulled to her chin as if to hide behind. 'I saw him out at the woods. He was one of them. He was one of the wolves.'

The man Karen Leigh had trusted to see Tara-May through her nightmares, to banish the ghosts of the dreams that haunted her, stood transformed. He'd straightened up, seeming to have grown another inch or two. And the way he handled that weapon now. . . .

'Guess you know the truth,' Landon Coyle said.

'You ain't denying it?' Ethan Hague made to move forward, casual like.

'Just you stay there, Deputy. I think I like you up against that wall beside the door. You'll do me the courtesy of remaining there.'

Hague shook his head. 'You'll never get away with this, Coyle.'

'I don't suppose so. But I know whatever happens to me in here, won't be anywhere near as bad as what the Black Wolf would do to me if I didn't kill our little witness.'

Eyes met, and the truth of his statement was clearly understood by everyone in the room. If this was to end, then it wouldn't be without bloodshed.

More pounding came from the door, again making everyone jump. The preacher laughed nervously. 'Boy, that breaks the tension, don't it?'

Gus Dudgeon's voice came through the door. 'Hey in there. I said to open up.'

'We got a situation, boss,' Ethan Hague called.

'You handling it?' the sheriff asked.

'Not too well.'

There was a pause, and then, 'I speak to Landon?'

'I'm afraid we've nothing to say to each other, Sheriff.'

'Landon, you don't have to do this. Whatever hold the Black Wolf's got on you, it won't mean nothing once we get his description and bring him in to trial.'

'You don't know how powerful he is, Sheriff. Has that train arrived with your portrait artist?' When there was no reply, the preacher said, 'You'll never capture him. Your artist is dead, which by my count makes two of them you tried to fetch in and two of them gone the same way. I'm sorry, but I have to do this.'

'You're gonna kill a little girl, man,' Ethan Hague spat. 'What God could countenance that?'

'It's nothing to do with God,' Coyle replied, and cast a glance over his shoulder to Tara-May, trapped and with no way out of her cell. 'It's just the way it has to be.'

Beads of sweat slicked his forehead. He was troubled at the thought of having to shoot a child, but Karen Leigh saw that he'd bring himself to do it. Her daughter was going to die. Ethan Hague must've seen that too. He leaped forward, aiming to get to the preacher and snatch the rifle. But he wasn't fast

120

enough and was hampered by the unwhirling bandage on his hand. Landon Coyle stepped back into the cell, swinging the rifle on to the deputy.

The roar from the weapon was deafening, the effect immediate on Ethan Hague. It hit him in the shoulder. He spun around, thrown off trajectory, flew into the bars of the second cell, crumpling to the ground as crimson speckles clouded the stone floor like flecks of rust.

For a moment all was stillness. And then Mainey Dudgeon moved across to him calling out his name, while Landon Coyle looked down at what he'd done. The pounding on the door began again, accompanied by yells. Tara-May called out for her ma. Her ma called her daughter's name, too.

'Shut up all of you!' the preacher yelled.

He spun around and the shadows in the cell seemed to unknit themselves to reveal the little girl cowering away from him. It was as if there was nothing else to do but put a bullet in her. Landon Coyle raised the weapon and took aim, pressed his finger to the trigger.

Another deafening roar filled the jailhouse.

CHAPTER 11

'Thank goodness,' Sam said. 'Somewhere to stay. It means we won't have to sleep out tonight, doesn't it, Will?'

'I'm not so sure about that,' Will said, studying the cabin.

'But no one lives in it, surely.'

'Maybe not. But the Deal Gang won't ease up on following us. I'm not sure we can stay here.'

'Well at least we can look inside and think about it.'

Will shrugged, which she took as permission to hunt around. The cabin was creeper-bound, almost hidden in the trees. If she hadn't stumbled around looking to find someplace to call a restroom (*I'll be grateful if I might step off this horse for a moment*, was how she'd told Will of her needs) they'd have passed right by without knowing it was there.

'The door's jammed,' she said, disappointed.

Sighing, Will left his horse and quit looking back

towards the trail they'd peeled off of for sign of Big Jim Deal. He put his shoulder against the rickety door and pushed. With a squeal, it opened inwards, releasing a musty, dry smell from its murky interior. Will pulled out his pistol and ducked inside. 'It's empty.'

'It'd protect us from the rain,' Sam said, seeing the roof was intact.

'Ain't gonna rain tonight.'

'The cold then.'

Will didn't say anything. He prowled around examining the walls, his boots clunking on the timber flooring. He kept his hat on, even though it must have stolen some of the light from his eyes. Sam watched him, wondering how she'd draw the man. Straight lines, she thought. With a sparseness to them. Leave the detail to a minimum. Just dots for his stubble, all suggestion and mystery. He'd be hard to capture, but she wanted to try.

She opened a small cupboard, found a candle and candleholder, and an old glass for drinking shots of whiskey out of. Nothing else. Unless you counted the mummified spider and the strands of a wispy web. Meanwhile, Will leaned over and picked some things up near the end of what had been a cot before rot had got to it. He shook them out.

'Oh no,' Sam said when she saw what he was holding out to her.

'They'll serve you better than that stuff you've got on now. Keep away the cold. We get going, it'll offer protection against the night and the cuts and grazes you're picking up.'

Sam looked at the checked shirt, the button bib coveralls he held. Knew he was right. All the same, her arms crossed her chest, as if he'd caught her stripped down bare. 'I'm not undressing in front of you,' she told him.

He nodded, hardly any expression visible under that hat he wore angled just so. 'I'll go see if there's any water nearby, take one of the horses. Got some planning to do.'

'Have you got a match before you go?' she said, showing him the candle. 'Anything to light the place up?'

He offered her his grin again, the one she couldn't decide she should be happy about or just plain ought to worry at.

Without the strips of the lady portrait artist's clothing, the trail was harder to follow. A couple of times they'd tracked back on themselves to find the path that'd eluded them. They were moving quickly, and because of that it was easy to miss a sign or to follow a false trail designed to stray them off the path they should be taking. 'He's figured we're coming after him,' stringy Pete Kingsley said.

Big Jim nodded. 'That's about the way I see it, too.'

He looked up to the sky, judging the time of day not by its hour but by how much light remained. 'They'll not ride overnight. Too dangerous. A horse puts a foot wrong, they could have a maimed animal on their hands. Worse than that, come to injury themselves. But they know we're after them. They'll want to hole up as far from us as they can manage.'

'Soon be sundown, boss,' Jack Kilkenny said, dark eyes seeing the pale moon, knowing that the stars would follow.

'We press on, catch up with them,' Big Jim said, thinking of what Will Tayling had done to his men on the train. 'Got us a reckoning to fix with our friend the Quiet One.'

So they rode. Into the coming night. Not a man objected, even when the day grew dangerously short of light as they climbed the trail up the valley side. And because they were checking false leads and fakery from the Quiet One, they happened upon the way down to the cabin that Will Tayling and Samantha Sloane had come across by accident.

'Shh, keep it quiet,' Big Jim said. He slid with barely a rustle from his saddle. His men followed suit, huddled around him. 'Recognize that horse?' He pointed a short distance from the cabin, where, just visible in the descending dusk, the animal had been tethered.

'Anders Finn's.'

'Uh huh.'

'So where's Tayling's grey mare?'

'Maybe he ain't here, only the lady artist is. See the light through the crack in the door. Someone's around. I'll lay money that he's left her, gone to get some firewood or else he's trying to set another false trail to lead us on to.'

'Then let's go in and get her, boss.'

Big Jim lifted a hand. 'Not so eager. Let's do this quietly, make sure we don't alert Tayling to what we're up to. The way I want it,' Big Jim said, 'I'm in there when he comes back. There's no sign of me on the way in. He comes along, ties up his horse, thinking he's done all he's needed to do to send us off into the mountains. Then he opens the door. He looks up, expecting to see his lady friend, and instead Big Jim's there, a Colt pistol pointing straight at his heart, his lady artist all trussed up, looking at him with her scared eyes.'

'Then we come in, boss, from behind, right?'

'Something like that. Tie him up, make him suffer. If I don't outright shoot him the second he walks in, on account of what he did to our guys.'

The outlaws scooted around, following Big Jim's directions, hugging the cabin walls to slink to the door. Big Jim, feeling that power he had, the guy who could summon thunder and make mountain cuts crumble and fall, stood back, sending his men in first to subdue the lady artist. He'd walk in theatrically, tell her who he was, Big Jim Deal, who's outsmarted Will Tayling, this hotshot Texas Ranger who arrested French Henry back in the day.

When the guys were ready, tight to the walls in case Tayling had left her a gun and she decided to defend herself, Big Jim nodded. He stood back a little way, so he could stride in as if he owned the place. 'Go ahead,' he whispered.

Parkins Whelks pushed on the door, shoving it real hard as it scraped along the floor. Jack Kilkenny eagerly rushed through to the lighted room inside, gun at the ready. Then there was the loudest and most unexpected sound of thunder Big Jim Deal had ever heard.

Will brought his horse to a halt, looked back over his shoulder. Sam Sloane, dressed up in her bib coveralls and second-hand logger's shirt, her arms wrapped around Will's torso as she sat behind him, jerked awake. She'd fallen asleep against his back, an ear pressed to his vest, hearing the reassuring thud of his heart.

Now she heard the aftermath of the explosion echo up the steep side of the tree-covered slopes. She saw a mushrooming ball of fire lift into the air. Crimson red, touch of burnt sienna, amber and yellow. That's what she'd use if she were to paint the scene, the pointed trees in dark blue over a Prussian blue wash. Salt the top of the paper first, so that it gave the effect of stars.

'Guess we've an idea where they got to,' Will said.

'Uh huh.'

'We can rest up now, get some sleep for the night.'

After the travelling she'd done, thinking of what lay ahead of her still – the morning journey to Autumn Jericho and the anxiety at the thought of having to sketch the Black Wolf – Sam didn't even complain that she'd be without a roof over her head tonight. She was just so achingly tired she'd happily sleep anywhere.

But while she slept peacefully, the folk of Autumn Jericho did anything but that.

The corpse of Landon Coyle had been removed, ushered away by the town's undertaker – a quiet job carried out with as much discretion as the man could manage, though of course the sound of shooting from the jailhouse hadn't gone unnoticed, nor passed by unspoken. In Paige Somerfield's saloon, while the piano played and bottles of beer were emptied, speculation about events spread. Tension threaded the town.

In the jailhouse, Karen Leigh held her daughter, whose silence was deep and as dense as the gathered night beyond the shutters. Karen hadn't spoken since she'd taken up Ethan Hague's pistol from the desk and put all the bullets it held into the back of Landon Coyle. Now she lay wrapped around her daughter on the little cot in the prison cell, wishing this nightmare would end.

Gus Dudgeon took his turn to keep watch and to feed the pot-bellied stove. When his shift was over, either Leo Enwright or Taylor Quinn sat for a spell, sometimes singly, sometimes in pairs, wary eyes going to the door, fearing the world beyond. None of them knew who they could trust and who they couldn't.

Gus had taken Mainey over to the saloon earlier, quietly leaving her in Paige's care for the night. Hugh Masters was there, as were a lot of other folk, all talking about the gunfire in the jail that afternoon. Joe Sullivan, who Gus had tried to deputize a couple of times without any luck, was on a barstool, Garth Brady beside him, somehow still standing despite all the drink he'd taken. Doc Grimshaw was there too; Doc, who'd patched up Ethan Hague pretty good, declaring, 'He'll live'. Ethan was in the jailhouse, snoozing, but before he dropped off, high on some kind of medicine, he was promising to shoot anyone the sheriff asked him to. The night pressed on towards midnight.

And then five horsemen rode through town, shooting into the air. They raced in from the outskirts, passing Maisey's stabling barns, right by the smithy and the wood workers, charging up Main Street toward the jailhouse. The jailhouse door burst open after bullets winged into the building. Rifle fire erupted after the riders. But they were gone and not a shot hit home.

They left something behind them, though, rolling to a stop in the dust after their horses.

Gus Dudgeon skipped down on to the street, turned the body over. It had been slit open, just as the body of Bucky Wright was slit open, just as the body of Patch Amory was slit open. Just as any other number of bodies had been slit open by anyone who'd crossed the Black Wolf. Trapper Joe this time.

Gus closed the man's staring eyes.

A shot rang out from the other end of Main Street. There, catching the light from the horned moon, the gleaming snout of the wolf mask revealing its white teeth, was the Black Wolf. Sure he'd been seen, he turned his stallion around and galloped off before Gus could swing his weapon on him.

CHAPTER 12

When Sam woke the sky had clouded over, but it was still light enough that the strengthening sun found some patches of blue to startle to brilliance.

It was just around dawn. You woke earlier sleeping outdoors, she figured.

She put a hand to her hair, clumped and matted where Will Tayling had gone at it with his curved knife yesterday. She didn't grieve for the missing hair. She couldn't have put up with another minute of catching it in the branches and snagging it on wildflowers growing through the trees and on the hooks of the thorny briars. Maybe she'd keep it short after today.

'Hey, Will, do you think—?' she said, and then stopped.

She'd been going to ask him if he thought she should keep her hair cut short, if it suited her. But Will wasn't about. The fire he'd set up last night, carefully building it in a circle of rocks on some hard earth, had dwindled and died. He'd been sleeping close by, head propped against his saddle, hat tilted even further over his eyes than usual.

Sam stood up, brushing off her borrowed clothes. The overalls didn't quite fit, and Will had suggested a bit of rope around the waist to bring it in there, turn up the legs so she wouldn't trip on them, but she had to admit he'd been right: they were more suitable for the outdoors than her bunchy skirt and blouse had been. 'Will?' she called. Wherever he'd gone, he'd gone barefoot, because his cowboy boots had been left by the fire. 'Will Tayling!'

But there was no reply. At least no reply she wanted to hear. Instead, a throaty chuckling came from behind her. She spun around. A dark and grubby hand fastened over her mouth and nose before she'd chance to scream. Sam kicked and rained punches against the broad girth of the man who'd hold of her. But he didn't feel any of it.

The monster tied her with the rope she was using for a belt, trussed her as she'd seen Anders Finn trussed on the train yesterday morning. Then he stuffed an old rag in her mouth.

When Will walked back to the small camp he was carrying a criss-crossed stack of dry wood. He was whistling, like he'd few cares to worry him. Any other time Sam would've been amazed, seeing him happy like that. But not now. She tried her best, wriggled and tugged on her bonds, crying out every bit as loud as she could manage from behind the obstruction in her mouth.

Will stopped as if he'd walked into an invisible wall, seeing her like that. But he wasn't stunned for long. He dropped the sticks, went for his pistol. . . .

. . . Only remembering at the last moment that his weapon was in his gun-belt, and that he'd removed it and tucked it up by the saddle he was making use of as a pillow through the night.

'Looks like you ain't got no weapons, Mister Texas Ranger,' the burned monster that had subdued Sam so effortlessly said. Even from where she lay, she could smell the smoke on him. He had to be the one Will had feared would catch them. Big Jim Deal. He'd somehow survived the explosion Will had set last night, though he'd not come through it unscathed.

Will adjusted his hat so it made the shadows work across his face. 'Looks like you had an accident setting up your camp-fire last night, Jim.'

'Weren't nothing to the accident you're about to have, Quiet One.' Jim Deal's voice was a throaty husk of what it must once have been.

'Takes more than dynamite to blow you up, huh?'

The burned flesh of his face made it impossible to tell if the big man was smiling or not. 'Took that from Henry, did you? The charges and settings? I shoulda known.'

'Figured it might come in handy.'

'You've cost me some good men, Tayling. I'm the only one left now. But it's enough. The reckoning

133

starts here.'

Will shook his head. 'We don't have to do this.'

'Yes we do.'

Without chewing on it any longer, the big man shuffled forward to meet Will around the ash of the camp-fire. He swung a hand as big as a rock toward Will's head. Will saw it coming and ducked, making sure to dance out of the way, hampered by being barefoot. 'You've slowed down, Jim,' he said.

The big man sounded to be hurting a lot. Sam wondered that he found the strength to stand, let alone fight. He was burned, his face a distortion of a man's face, what were left of his sooty clothes had tears in them; blood oozed out of wounds across his abdomen. He must've been climbing the trail after them throughout the night, and still he hadn't run out of energy, despite that heavy wheezing from both his mouth and his chest.

'Only have to catch hold of you once, then it's all over.'

'It's already over, Jim. Sam and me, we're going to Autumn Jericho, put the Black Wolf out of business. He won't be able to help you. You're finished.'

'No!' Big Jim roared, his face a blackened fury, and from somewhere neither Will nor Sam had anticipated, he found the energy to fly at Will.

Before Will could leap back, he was caught in a bear hug, the pair rolling into the sparse grass lining the side of the trail. They sank into a ditch, sounds of fighting following.

Sam wriggled to watch what was happening, wishing she could break free of her bindings and get a weapon.

Will flew into the camp, landing on his back, the air knocked out of him. His hat had come off, which, for an absurd moment, Sam thought would hurt him more than Jim Deal's punches. Will shook his head just as Jim lumbered over to him. Jim leaned down, wheezing even more, and, snatching him up by his shirt drove his forehead into Will's face. Will slumped even further, lolled groggily as the big man held him upright and butted him again. Big Jim laughed, even though it caused him pain to do so. 'Mister hotshot Ranger.'

Will murmured something.

'What's that?' Jim said, leaning in close.

Will took his chance, drove his forehead into Big Jim's nose. Blood spat out in twin gushers, and in that moment of the big man's pain and surprise, Will grabbed hold of his chest, seeking the spot where he'd figured the wheezing to be coming from. He found a tear of flesh and dug his fingers in, feeling whatever was lodged there press deeper and get stickier – wood from the cabin when it had exploded, maybe, puncturing Jim's lung.

Jim Deal howled in pain, as much as a man with a voice ripped hoarse of air can do.

Will staggered away from him, over to the saddle and his gun-belt. Without ceremony, he unhitched his pistol and swung it up at Jim Deal, shooting him dead when the burned man turned around to charge at him for the final time. Even as Jim Deal fell, Sam saw Will pluck out the knife he kept in his boot, to come cut her free of her bonds.

Gus Dudgeon was pleased to see dawn. The wolves had raced through the town six, maybe seven times last night, shooting in the air on each occasion, whooping and a-hollering so that it was impossible for anyone to get a lick of sleep. There was no pattern to when they'd ride in. Sometimes it was an hour between their raids, other times just minutes. On what had proved to be their last couple of runs, they'd loosed shots at the jailhouse too, bullets thwacking into the shutters and doors but not passing through.

While Gus was pleased Mainey had relented to spending the night over at Paige Somerfield's saloon, the wolves' raids hadn't made for a pleasant time in the jailhouse, and the little girl they were so depending on was frightened half to death. Seeing the tension getting to her, he'd called time on going out shooting after the Black Wolf's men.

'Stay inside. We're safe behind these walls. We only go out if they try burn us up.'

So the wolves had the run of the town; house doors stayed locked and bolted, lamps doused and people hid in their beds, worrying at what had befallen Autumn Jericho, wondering why the law stayed locked up in its own jailhouse.

136

And then dawn had arrived, finally, pinking the eastern sky. Somehow – and Gus Dudgeon wasn't really sure how – they'd made it through the night. He sent a prayer of thanks up for that one, hoping it went to a different god from the one Landon Coyle worshipped; and then, maybe pushing his luck, he asked for another favour too. To his surprise, in a few hours that one was met as well.

A grey mare rode into town, two figures on its back. The tall man on front of the horse, who was dressed in grey and had his hat pulled down, didn't rush his horse. He just kept on riding, passing the smaller houses, and then moved in by the stabling barns, nodding politely to anyone who stopped to look at him and the passenger behind him. He steered that horse up past the dry goods store, carried on past Jim Salmon the barber's, casting an eye across to the big red-brick building of the town bank, before sauntering on by Paige Somerfield's saloon until he drew to a stop ten yards from the jail-house.

Seeing it was locked up tight, the shutters firmly closed and the door resolutely shut, he turned and said something to his passenger – not a boy as some had mistakenly thought on first seeing the stubble-haired blonde in the bib overalls and checked lumberjack's shirt, but a young woman – and she seemed to shake herself awake, nod and then speak into his ear, just under the brim of that hat he was wearing canted at its unlikely angle. The man took in what the woman had said to him and thought about it for some time. Then he called out, 'Hey there, in the jailhouse.'

The first sounds of the day came from the building. Bolts scraped back, a key twisted loudly, a lock squealed. The door opened. Stepping into the midday light, a mighty relieved smile on his face, came the sheriff. He jumped off the porch, easing a back stiffened through the night's watch, looked on by the jailer, Leo Enwright. Leo stood there with his beady eyes alert for danger as he cradled an old shotgun in his hands. Gus helped the young woman down and rushed her and the wooden box she carried into the jailhouse.

The grey man, tying up his horse outside the sheriff's office, went in after them. The door slammed shut and the bolts and locks went into place again.

The light wasn't great, and her witness was . . . well, not uncooperative, but real tricky to get to grips with. The urgency with which both of them were expected to come up with something wasn't helping either. The tension was in the air, like the buzz in the atmosphere come an electrical storm.

Sam tried to lighten the mood. 'Well, let's see what we can sketch now, shall we? Then we can do some drawing together, I'll teach you. We can draw some horses, maybe.'

'Patsy-Ann.'

'All right,' Sam said, with no idea who Patsy-Ann was. 'We'll draw Patsy-Ann when I teach you. That'd be nice.' Dipping into her artist's materials, Sam pulled out a bottle of ink and diluted some of it with water, took out a quill with a hard-nib. She angled her paper, trying to catch some of the light from the lantern beside her. It was dark in the cell, but the little girl wouldn't come out, and insisted her mother remain with her.

'Why's your hair like that?' the little girl asked.

Sam pulled a face. 'You like it?'

'Dunno.'

'I dunno if I like it either. Tell me about the man you saw, when he took his mask off.'

Tara-May hid her face in her hands, burrowed into her mother, who seemed not too much less vacant than the daughter. This was going to take some time. While Sam tried to coax the girl into giving her a description, at last making a start, she saw Will Tayling in a huddle with the sheriff and his deputies, no doubt bringing them up to speed on all that had happened on the journey to Autumn Jericho. The men were talking quietly and seriously.

Slowly, the portrait began to take shape, and the more involved she became in it, the less Tara-May was frightened of the image forming on the paper. Instead, she was more concerned about getting the details correct, so that the picture was right. Sam had to start again twice, but each time she did she was sure they were closer to capturing the Black Wolf's likeness.

'Oh, honey,' the girl's mother said with a sigh, once Sam had shown the child the final picture. 'You're getting confused. That can't be him.'

'But it is, I swear it, Ma.'

Hearing the commotion, the sheriff came into the cell. 'You all about done? Because if you are, we can set about getting some posters made up from the picture.'

Leo Enwright, the kindly old guy who looked like he'd come across on the *Mayflower*, took the portrait from Tara-May's mother, held it to the light so he could squint at it better.

'Well, I'll be,' he murmured.

'It's true. It's him. I don't understand what I've done wrong,' Tara-May said.

The sheriff looked at the image Leo showed him, then to Sam. She shrugged. 'It's what she told me to draw, Sheriff. You know this man?'

'Rightly I do. He's a little bit . . . effete, my wife Mainey calls him. But you know, there's always been something about him I've never been keen on, like he's secretly laughing at you. He's tall enough and of a frame to match the Wolf, at least as much of him as we've ever seen. And he's a wealthy man too, though I don't know how he came by that wealth. Always helping fund the churches and—' The sheriff stopped.

'Funding the churches,' Leo said. 'That's how he was into Landon Coyle.'

'The girl's right,' said the sheriff. 'It's him. He's an

140

alderman, knows all about us getting a lead on the Black Wolf because I told him at the last town meeting. He obviously sought out more information, learned we had a witness after that. Let's saddle up and bring him in, before he's wise to the fact we're on to him. Without Coyle as an informer he must be getting spooked. He won't know what's going on. Maybe we can catch him unawares, have him in irons before the travelling judge's due in town.'

Gus led Taylor Quinn and Leo Enwright out on to the porch, rifles loaded. Will Tayling came after them. 'Deputy Hague's fit enough to shoot from in there,' he told Gus. 'The women don't need me to look after them. So I'm thinking you could use a hand.'

'I ain't gonna say no, Will. Not to you. You know that.'

'Then if you know where this guy lives, let's get a move on.'

They were prevented from going to the horses (though by rights, Leo would be taking the cart, his saddle-riding days long since done with) by a voice calling to them. Gus turned to see what the problem was. Paige Somerfield hurried toward them, moving briskly in her fine dress, cleavage rolling noticeably in front of her, a hard thing for any man not to appreciate.

'Heck, we ain't got time for none of your old flames, Sheriff,' Leo said, and spat out some tobacco.

'Something's wrong.' Gus felt a disquieting and

violent illness in his stomach. He went to the woman, meeting her halfway across the street. 'What is it, Paige? Tell me.'

'It's Mainey, Sheriff.' The fact she was calling him Sheriff and there was no teasing in her voice told him enough. 'She's gone. Wasn't in her room this morning, and the bed had hardly been slept in. But there was this, on her pillow. . . .'

She held out with some distaste the object she'd covered in the latest edition of the one-sheet Autumn Jericho newspaper. Gus unwrapped it swiftly, aghast at what he saw.

A wolf's paw. Perfectly black.

CHAPTER 13

Will spared his horse, rode shotgun with Leo Enwright on the cart the old-timer had requisitioned, following Gus Dudgeon and Taylor Quinn. They travelled west along a big road that narrowed to a single-track trail, passing strong maples and rich farmland. This Hugh Masters, aka the Black Wolf, had chosen a beautiful part of the countryside to set himself up in, Will thought. With his lawman's eye, he saw how secluded it was out here. The perfect hideout for a criminal.

Gus slowed to a canter. Quinn had his horse fall into step with him, and Leo slowed the wagon. The old crate rattled loudly, but they'd draw to a stop before the cart's noises gave them away.

'We nearly there?' Will asked Leo, having to raise his voice to be heard.

'Good as,' the jailer said.

Will studied him, the stooped back, his wiry white beard, eyes squinting out from under an old prospector's hat. 'You didn't have to come,' Will said.

'No, I didn't. But the sheriff's a good man. His wife's a mighty fine woman. I couldn't have borne being back at the jailhouse, knowing I might be helping out here. Tell you something else – Ethan Hague, if it'd been possible, he'd've dragged himself here too if someone didn't have to look after the women.'

Will nodded, adjusting his hat after the bumpy ride on the wagon, saw as he did so that Gus was motioning them to stop, they were close enough. The rest of the way they'd go on foot.

Hugh Masters' house was a big sprawling ranch-type affair. Its bottom storey was made out of stone, with a wooden porch and a veranda. Up above that a widow's walk circled the upper timber floor, both walk and wood painted cream. The roof was peaked and tiled and an ornate lightning conductor-cum-weather vane turned as the wind caught it, sending a low grinding sound to where Gus Dudgeon and his men were hidden. Otherwise all was silent. It looked like there wasn't a soul at home.

'There's no one protecting the place; let's go,' Taylor Quinn said. 'What're we waiting for?'

'Too quiet,' Leo Enwright said.

'I agree,' Gus said.

'Whaddaya mean, it's too quiet?'

'A day like today, there should be someone moving around. Look at that, no doors are open. You can't see anyone inside either. I think they're expecting us. Word must've carried from town that a couple of strangers have been seen in the jailhouse.' Meaning Will and Sam. 'Must've realized there'd soon be a picture of the Wolf.'

Will Tayling came back from his sortie so deftly he was upon them before they'd much chance to react. Gus Dudgeon was the only one had time to spring around and level his rifle at him.

Holding a gloved hand up, Will motioned that it was all right. 'Only me,' he said.

'What did you see?'

'The whole house is like this. They're staying cooped up in there. But I glimpsed one guy at a window. He was armed. A rifle. Was watching out for anyone approaching.'

'Hugh Masters?'

'I don't think so.'

'Then he's got his men here. Fixed up for a gun-fight if it comes to it.'

'Wolves,' Leo said, tightening his grip on his shotgun. He spat into the undergrowth. 'We'll shoot them like animals.'

'Not so fast. Remember my wife's in there. We can't just blast them out. Have to sneak in somehow and rescue her.'

None of them said what they were thinking: they could only rescue her if she was still alive.

'Any thoughts about how we get in?' Gus said.

Will skidded the back of his hand across his chin. 'The direct approach, I reckon. You think, Leo?'

'Hey now. You smiling at me like that for?' Leo Enwright said.

The cart rolled up the driveway, making for the turning circle in front of the Masters house.

'I surely don't like this,' Leo whispered. 'I surely don't.'

But no one fired on him. The house just stood there, not a sign of movement in it. The turn of the cart's wheels, the clump of the horses' hoofs, and the usual creaks from the vehicle were the only noises as he pulled up.

'Easy now,' he said, aware of how exposed he was. It was all he could do not to glance down at his shotgun, hidden beneath his buckskin jacket, which he'd draped seemingly casually on the seat beside him. When the dust had settled now he'd come to a stop, he waited. But no one came out to greet him.

'Hey in there,' he yelled. Shoulda brought his old hunting horn, might've done some good in rousing someone. 'Hey!'

When still no one put in an appearance, Leo fished in his pants pocket, brought out a bunch of small stones, which he'd picked up just for this situation. Selecting a biggish one, he threw it at the door. Watched it ping off the porch upright. 'Goddamn. Never could throw straight.'

For the next few minutes he tossed stones at the door, sure someone was watching. Whatever the inadequacies of his aim, he finally got a result from it. The door opened and two men, dressed head to foot in black, sidled out on to the porch. Both carried rifles over their shoulders. 'Help you, old-timer?' one said. 'Because there's no call for you to be on this property I can think of.'

'I'm here to pick up a guest of Mister Masters,' Leo said, not liking being called an old-timer by this ugly pup. 'And I'll ask you to call me sir when you speak to me, young fella.'

The guy smirked, glanced at his companion.

'Ain't nobody staying here with Mister Masters. You been sent out on a fool's errand. Why don't you just git, old-timer, sir.'

'Well now. I cain't rightly do that. See, Sheriff Dudgeon,' the two men jerked at the sheriff's name, 'he told me to come on over here to pick up his wife. Seems that Mister Masters is the Black Wolf, you know, that outlaw character, and the sheriff said I was to shoot dead anyone who got in the way of me.'

'The heck?' the second man in black said, as the first advanced from the porch toward Leo.

Just then glass broke, flying outward, and another black-garbed figure came tumbling out of an upstairs window, rolled off the top of the veranda and crashed down dead by the shrubbery lining the porch.

'Ambush!' the first man in black cried, lifting his rifle toward Leo.

From the back of the cart, springing up from where he'd been hidden, Taylor Quinn picked him off with a bullet from his rifle and swung around to take the other wolf out, not a shot wasted, two bullets: two dead men. He'd done the job while Leo was still trying to untangle his shotgun from his buckskin jacket. Now he leaped off the cart, and pounded up the porch steps to stand to one side of the main door. He ducked his head around to look in, seeing that the way was clear, and then disappeared inside.

'Heck an' bean stacks,' Leo complained, scuttling after him with his shotgun and spare cartridges. 'Wait for me, now.'

Things went wrong after Will and Gus had cold-cocked a couple of guys on the back door (set up as guards there, they'd been distracted by Leo arriving out front, so it was easy work to take them down) and made their way to a broad flight of stairs. They reasoned that if Mainey was being held anywhere in the building, it would be on the second storey. Harder to get to, harder to escape from, easier to defend. So far they hadn't had to fire a single shot, had come in unnoticed.

'Feel too easy to you?' Gus whispered as they passed through the hallway.

'Yeah, but I'll take easy after the twenty-four hours I've had.'

'Same here.' Gus nodded. 'The stairs.'

They went up deftly for a couple of big guys. Then right on the final stair the tread creaked under Will's boot. The sound was enough to draw the attention of the fair-haired wolf who'd been glancing out the window to see what the old coot on the horse and cart was after. As luck would have it, the wolf noticed Taylor Quinn laying flat out on the bed of the cart, rifle at the ready, round about the same time Will set the stair creaking, and turning around expecting one of the other wolves, he'd frozen, taking in the expressions on the intruders' faces.

By then Gus was racing at him. The wolf yelled and fumbled for his weapon, coming forward to meet the sheriff. Gus caught the man easily, despite his strong build, prevented him drawing and slammed his own pistol into the guy's face. But the guy wouldn't go down. 'Tough skull,' Gus complained to Will as the wolf yelled, wrestling him.

'Just shut him up,' Will hissed.

Realizing their cover had been blown, Gus figured he'd help Leo and Taylor Quinn out while disposing of the problem struggling in his grip. He spun around, propelling the wolf at the window, pitched him straight through the glass.

'Subtle,' Will said when the crashing and thumps of the falling wolf died down.

Gus shrugged. 'You were the one made the noise on the stair.'

The shooting started below.

'OK, quick. Split up. Me there, you there.' Gus pointed down first one corridor, and then sent Will the other way.

Will had to take out two wolves racing toward him.

149

Then his rifle jammed. A third nearly used that to his advantage, but his aim was poor, his shot crashing into the wall beside Will. By then Will had tossed the rifle away, had drawn – nobody was quicker pulling a Colt than Will Tayling – and fanned the hammer twice, bringing the third wolf down. The way was clear.

He checked the rooms along the corridor, found storage spaces, bedrooms, even a small library. But there was no sign of Mainey Dudgeon or Hugh Masters. From the downstairs rooms there was more shooting, and it sounded like weapons firing on the veranda. Will heard Leo Enwright's big dirty shotgun discharge and the old hoss's laughter afterwards. At least someone was having fun, Will thought. He was going to return and see how Gus was getting on, but saw a pair of wolves run up the stairs. There must've been ten, maybe more, in the house. These guys looked like the ones Will and Gus had knocked out when they broke in. Seeing Will they sprayed rounds at him, all striking the doorway he stood in.

The angle was wrong for Will to return fire, being left-handed, so ducking into the room he slammed the door shut, ran over to the window and slid it up. He clambered out on to the widow's walk and, staying low, scooted around the house on the outside. As he went a section of the deck exploded just behind him, and Leo Enwright yelled up, 'Darn it. Run, you wolf critter. Get you next time.'

'It's me, Leo,' Will yelled. 'Don't shoot.'

'Haw! Sorry, fella.'

Will heard windows sliding up, the wolves looking for him. He spun around and took one out, while the other ducked inside, leaving only his arm out, waving a pistol in something like Will's direction. Bullets flew by, aimed randomly. But it only took one, Will knew. . . .

He ran, heading for the corner of the house, stumbled just as a bullet whanged into his pistol – a shot the guy shooting at him could never have made if he'd been trying – and snatched it from his hand. Will didn't stop, made it around the corner of the house in a dive. He scrambled up, kept running. He might not have a gun, but he wasn't going to surrender. He doubted that was an option left anyway. He was just pleased he'd all of his fingers.

Had to be careful from here on in without a firearm. He slowed at the final window along the widow's walk, which by his reckoning was the last room along the corridor Gus Dudgeon had headed down. There'd been some shooting from along here; Will had heard it as he'd let his own gun do his talking, but now he judged all the weapons fire to be coming from downstairs. Leo's shotgun was an unmistakable explosion every twenty seconds or so. And Taylor Quinn was trading shots with yet more wolves. But it was awful quiet up here.

Sensing things weren't right, Will edged over to the window. He even went so far as to take his hat off so he could peer inside without anyone in the room noticing him.

Gus Dudgeon saw Will. No one else did. Not his wife Mainey, who was tied up and unable to move, and not Hugh Masters, wearing his Black Wolf mask, who held her locked tight by the throat between himself and Gus's pistol.

'Telling you for the last time, Masters,' Gus said, not giving away he'd seen Will at the window. 'You let her go now.'

The Black Wolf held a gleaming knife in his hand – hooked like the claw of a wolf, Gus supposed it was meant to be. It didn't take much figuring to associate that knife with the wounds on folk who'd crossed the Wolf or posed a danger to him. Most recently, of course, Patch Amory the artist and Trapper Joe. Gus wouldn't be surprised to learn Joe's dogs had met their end by way of that blade either.

'Or what, Sheriff?' the Black Wolf snarled. 'You've been shot. How long before you run out of blood and collapse on the floor?'

'Yeah, I've been hit,' Gus said, as much for Will's benefit as anything, letting him know the state of things in here. 'But your men now, your wolves, they're getting shot up pretty badly too, I reckon. Far worse than me. Any minute now, ain't gonna be no one alive in this house but me and my deputies. In case you ain't figured it out, our witness got the artist to draw you up pretty accurately, Masters. Your boys in the hills, they failed to stop that portrait artist. A titchy little girl she is, too.'

The Wolf seemed enraged by this news. He brought the knife closer to Mainey's neck. Her eyes widened in fright, then slammed shut.

'Hold it now,' Gus said, and did his best not to cringe at the pain he felt from the gunshot he'd taken. It was a deep wound, at the top of his thigh, but although he was weeping blood and found it hard to stay standing, he didn't think he was leaking enough to drop dead just yet. He was down to one pistol, holding the blood in with his other hand, but his aim didn't waver.

The Wolf paused, and the sound of the gunfire from downstairs died down. The situation in the room remained unchanged. But footsteps sounded nearby, a final couple of shots rang out, and then voices called, 'Sheriff? Sheriff?'

'You see,' Gus Dudgeon told the Black Wolf. 'Your men are done with.'

'Maybe,' the Wolf admitted. 'But as long as I hold my prize here, I'm the one going to call the shots.'

The door opened and Taylor Quinn came through, sighting down his rifle. Leo Enwright followed a moment later, brushing his forehead clean of sweat.

'What'll we do, Sheriff?' Taylor Quinn asked, weapon on the wolf mask and the gleaming eyes within it.

The Wolf turned his snarling snout to the deputy.

153

'You should be asking me that question. The only way I'm not gonna cut up the sheriff's wife here is if you toss your guns on to that bed there. You do that, then the sheriff's gonna lay down his Colt too and you're all gonna back up against that wall.'

'And if we don't?' Leo Enwright said.

'I kill her and you kill me.'

'Why, I—'

'Do what he says,' Gus Dudgeon said.

'Are you crazy, Sheriff? You know what he's gonna do, don't you? He's gonna hold on to Mainey, then circle around and pick up a gun, shoot the three of us.'

Mainey Dudgeon clearly thought the same; she tried shaking her head, urging Gus not to follow the Wolf's commands. 'You're gonna have to trust me,' Gus said, hoping Will Tayling was picking up on this outside.

Somewhat resentfully, Leo tossed his shotgun on to the bed after Taylor Quinn laid out his rifle and pistols. They stood against the wall the Wolf waved them to. 'Good, good,' the Wolf said. 'Now you, Sheriff.'

'You won't hurt her?'

'I'll give her straight to you, Sheriff, soon as you've put your Colt where I told you.'

With exaggerated care, Gus let his weapon drop to the bed's plush covers, and moved back to the wall where Quinn and Enwright were standing. The Black Wolf edged over to the guns, Mainey between himself and the law, still his hostage. He passed by the window where Gus had seen Will as he did so. At the last, he pushed Mainey forward, and reached down to grab a pistol from the sheets.

Gus caught his wife, taking the strain on his good leg, and yelled, 'Head out the door!' as the Wolf spun around with a weapon raised, fixing to take a shot at the men.

Taylor Quinn ducked low, lifting Leo Enwright up and flinging him at the open door to the corridor outside, following on himself. Gus tried to do the same with Mainey, but she was still bound, a more awkward figure. She fell short of safety and he collapsed after her, a hand going to the open wound on his leg, which was seeping blood now he'd released the pressure on it.

Grinning, Hugh Masters plucked the wolf mask from his head. 'Just so you can see the face of the man who killed you and your wife, Sheriff,' he said, and sighted down the pistol.

Will Tayling flew through the window, straight into him. Will's own knife, plucked from the back of his boot, was in his left hand. He intended to damage the Black Wolf in the way the Wolf had done to so many others. Will was as swift as ever. Before the shower of broken glass and splintered wood that'd burst into the room with him had hit the floor, he plunged the knife into the man. Masters froze in shock, too astonished to even let out a scream as Will drew the blade up and spread an opening for his dark life to spill out of.

The Wolf didn't get a single bullet off before he died.

CHAPTER 14

Sam guided the little girl's hand as she drew the final line. 'There,' she said. 'How's that?'

'Patsy-Ann!' Tara-May sang, and showed the picture to her mother. Karen Leigh smiled. But it was a strained smile. Both women knew this wouldn't be over until the men returned, the Black Wolf captured and standing before the travelling judge or else put down in his home.

Ethan Hague, their protector, was snoozing on the one good easy chair. He was bandaged up around his shoulder, a rifle across his knees. Neither Sam nor Karen Leigh felt the urge to awaken him.

Just when they thought they couldn't bear the wait any longer, a series of quick knocks – 'It's the right code,' Karen Leigh said – sounded on the jailhouse door. Sam watched her open it up, sliding the bolts back and twisting the key.

Taylor Quinn walked, in, kicking the boots of Ethan Hague. The injured deputy woke up startled, the new light from the open door hitting his eyes. 'Man, that hurts,' he complained, raising a hand across his face.

'Was it all. . . ?' Karen Leigh asked.

'It's done; the Wolf's finished with, and we're all fine,' Gus Dudgeon said, limping into the jailhouse with his wife, pale and shaken, but very much alive, beside him. He fished out his chair from behind his desk and had her sit down. Then he leaned against the desk himself. Spots of blood were showing through a strip of fabric he'd wrapped around his upper thigh. But he waved the wound off when questioned about it. 'Doc's coming over to take a look, but it's nothing but a scratch. Say, it's dark in here, open up them shutters, someone.'

Taylor Quinn moved to do it.

As Tara-May pawed at her to draw something else, Sam asked, 'Is Will all right too?'

'He's right here, ma'am,' the sheriff said, as the tall, thin figure of Will Tayling followed Leo Enwright into the building.

'Howdy,' Will said, giving her that smile she still wasn't sure about. He looked tired, but he was alive, and that's all Sam realized she cared about right now.

Tara-May said, 'Draw something else now. Draw something different.'

Will nodded, meeting Sam's eye. 'Sure, go ahead and draw something.'

'How about I draw you,' Sam said.

Will Tayling, the former Texas Ranger, rubbed at

his chin, making the bristles rasp. She watched him think on her invitation, and then he said, 'Do I have to take my hat off?'